A HONEY OF A HOSTAGE

Spur was ready behind a big cottonwood tree when Rogers rode up. He swore and slowed. Spur aimed carefully with the Winchester. The girl sat astride behind Rogers, her arms locked around his chest, her skirt riding up to her waist.

At this angle McCoy could hit Rogers without endangering the girl. Spur refined his aim. Rogers stopped for a moment.

Spur fired.

The round hit Rogers in the left shoulder, away from the girl. He nearly fell off the horse but held on. He grabbed the girl with his good right hand, and crashed through the brush with his mount and pounded down the road.

"I'll kill her if you try to shoot at me again!"

Also in the Spur series:

SPUR #24

Dodge City Doll

Dirk Fletcher

LEISURE BOOKS NEW YORK CITY

A LEISURE BOOK

Published by

Dorchester Publishing Co., Inc.
6 East 39th Street
New York, NY 10016

Printed in the United States of America

Dodge City Doll

1

The polished derringer lifted again aiming at the sheriff's chest. His hand came up weakly, his voice only a whisper now as the pain eroded his strength.

"Why? For God's sakes. Why are you trying to kill me? I don't even know you! I've never done anything to you or yours. Do you get some wild kind of thrill from this?"

Sheriff Clyde Wilson touched his belly where only a small spot of blood showed through his pants. The first shot, which caught him totally by surprise, sliced into his lower abdomen, ripped through the intestines and lodged somewhere near his spine.

Damn, it hurt! He'd never experienced anything like it. Gut shot was not the way to cash out of a game.

"Give me just one reason, damnit!" he roared, the pain flooding over him again, dulling his vision. "Just one reason why. I deserve to know why you're killing me. Maybe I'm not the man you want. I know damn well I've never hurt you!" His voice faded to nothing as a surge of blinding pain started in his bowels and grew and grew as it billowed and splashed and bored its way through his body until it hit his brain and he cried out in agony, sure that he was dying.

A moment later, to his shock, he discovered he was still alive and he hurt as much as before. He shook his head and opened his eyes.

The twin muzzles of the little gun came closer. He didn't have the strength to lift his hand, let alone knock the small weapon away. But the derringer had already wounded him grievously, fatally, if he didn't get help soon.

The two figures sat in a closed black buggy at the edge of town. Both were dressed conservatively, a silver star shining on the sheriff's chest.

"Damnit, tell me why!" Sheriff Wilson gasped and shuddered. He lunged across the buggy but met only the muzzle of the derringer as it discharged. The .45 caliber slug rammed through his dark coat, shattered a rib and plunged in three pieces into his heart, killing him instantly.

The buggy swayed as someone got out. A slap on the horse's hind quarters sent it skittering away down the lane out of town.

Spur McCoy sat in the town marshal's office in Kimberly, Kansas, about six miles west of Wichita. He had picked up his orders in the larger town at the telegraph office, scanned his directions from Washington, D.C., the headquarters of the Secret Service and just made it on the stage heading west.

"Just heard about Clyde Wilson this morning," Marshal Paul Sanderson said. "Damn, known Clyde now for twenty years. He was a good lawman. You say it's happened before?"

"He's the fourth lawman to be murdered around here in the last four weeks. Three of them have been on the stage line heading for Dodge City. You're the new marshal here, I'd reckon."

"Right, the new marshal. I'm not quite used to that title yet."

"This is the first place a lawman was killed in this string. I'm investigating all the murders. Some people think that the same person or persons may be doing all of them."

"Somebody with a big hatred for lawmen?"

"Happens."

"Sure as hell does, McCoy. How can I help?"

An hour later McCoy had checked over a report by the undertaker who was also the county coroner. Death came as a result of a shot to the heart by a large caliber slug, probably a .45. There was a second gunshot wound in the lower abdomen with considerable bleeding. One curious fact recorded. Both wounds showed "severe powder burns indicating the weapon had been extremely close to the victim when shot."

Marshal Sanderson scratched his jaw. "Wasn't like Marshal Jones to be careless. He'd been town lawman here for ten years. Never a lot of trouble. We ain't a big cattle town like some of them. But Larabee Jones was a careful man."

"Where was he found?" Spur asked.

"Out along East River Road. He was in a buggy, not his own, and the horse was walking free, like nobody had tied the reins. The old black was just munching away on spring grass when we finally found Larabee."

"So he could have been shot anywhere and the horse driven or chased out there or maybe it wandered."

"Peers as how."

"Not much help."

"Happened near a month ago, and we ain't got a thing, not a clue and no suspects. Nobody heard nothing. Widow Jones said her husband didn't have no enemies she knew of. He didn't gamble or carouse with the fancy ladies. Marshal Jones was a short, kind of fat little man. Never raised his voice. Not one to pick a fight or hold a grudge. Funny kind of man to be a lawman, but he was a good one. Whole thing is a blamed mystery to us, Mr. McCoy."

"Well, keep it open, Marshal. I'm moving on down the line, see if I can get a line on the killer and stop him. Bad for the way people think about lawmen if somebody keeps killing us off all the time."

The remark brought a wry smile from Marshal Sanderson. "Hope that same polecat don't come back this way looking for another lawman to do in."

Spur waved and caught the afternoon stage for the next small town, River Run, fourteen miles down the road.

Another lawman had been murdered here, six days after the first one. Spur went through the same routine. The case of death was listed as two .45 rounds, one belly, one heart. It wasn't hard to figure which one had been fired first. There were intense powder burns around both wounds.

Again, there were no known enemies. The sheriff

was respected, ran a good office, was fair, did his job and kept the town as clean as possible. Yet somebody met him in a black carriage, shot him so close that powder burns were deep. One wound in the belly looked as if the muzzle of the weapon had been pressed against the man's pants as the weapon was fired.

Boys going to school found the buggy the next morning, the horse cropping grass in the small public park. No one had remembered seeing the rig the previous night. It belonged to the doctor and had been left in front of his place after a house call. He forgot to move it.

Back in his hotel room, Spur looked at his reports. He had missed the stage; he'd get he next one in the morning. The first two victims were found in buggies. Both had powder burns. Which meant it had been an up close job.

After seeing the results of the first two kills, Spur decided it was the work of the same man. No two people with a killing rage would kill two lawmen exactly the same way. It was one guy, but who and why and where was he now?

The next day he took the morning stage and covered the other two towns where lawmen had been murdered. He found the identical pattern. Death came from two .45 slugs, one to the belly and a second in the heart. One lawmen had scratches on his face. He was found a half mile out of town at the side of the road. The fourth lawman to die was in a buggy as well, parked in front of his own jail.

No suspects, no witnesses, no clues. The new lawmen in each town were at a loss to explain the killings, nor could they offer any idea who could be responsible. They agreed it probably wasn't a local man.

By now every lawman in the state of Kansas had been sent a flyer warning him about the danger from person or persons unknown. There had been no robberies or other killings in the towns so affected. The only motive seemed to be hatred for lawmen of all kinds. The sheriffs and marshals were warned to be on the lookout for any suspicious characters.

Spur looked at the map in the sheriff's office. There was only one direction the killer could go, on west, on down the stage road. Four killings so far, the last one here just two days ago. If he was lucky he could prevent the next one, but what town would it be in?

He picked the next biggest town down the line. That was Greensburg. County seat, with a sheriff and nearly twenty miles from this spot on the map. The killer might stop before there, or go past the town, it was a chance he'd have to take.

Perhaps he could stop a killing this time and nail a killer.

The stage came in on time and they got away quickly. As they neared the next stop several hours later, Spur's pulse picked up and he looked forward to the confrontation. He had a feeling that this was the right town, that something would happen here.

In was his job to stop the killing and to nail the killer.

He slid out of the coach, caught his carpetbag off the top of the rig and walked toward the hotels. He saw two of them, and from habit picked the best one, a three story affair called Pride of the Plains Hotel. It was to be hoped.

Spur McCoy stood taller than the average man at six feet two inches. His best fighting weight was two hundred pounds even, which made him slightly on the thick side, but it was all toned muscle, no fat. His reddish brown hair touched his shirt collar but was usually covered with a low crowned, gray Stetson. The sandy hair extended down almost to his jawline in mutton chop sideburns fronted with a full moustache of the same shade.

He stared out at the world through curious green eyes and was an excellent shot with pistol and rifle, was murder with a shotgun, and could ride as well as most cowboys but not as well as the Comanches or Sioux.

During the big war he had served in the infantry, rose to the rank of captain, took one small wound, and retired to Washington, D.C., where he was an aide to the senior senator from New York, an old family friend.

When the Secret Service was created by congress in 1858, he had been one of the first members of the force. It was originally started to defend and protect the currency against counterfeiting, but soon its scope broadened into general law work, especially where there were no other federal law officers to handle disputes across state lines.

Spur served in Washington for six months, then won the job as agent in charge of the western region, from St. Louis to the Pacific Coast.

His direct boss was General Wilton D. Halleck, the number two man in Washington who gave him his assignments through the wonders of the telegraph.

Boss of the operation was William Wood, the director of the Agency who had been appointed by Abraham Lincoln and by each President since.

Deep in his traveling kit, Spur carried an identification card that had been signed by President Lincoln, and a pair of carefully worded letters from General Halleck that made him a full colonel in the army and the orders to take over any military equipment or personnel he needed. Those letters were hidden between the covers of a book, carefully taped together.

He usually worked undercover, using a variety of names, since his real name was quickly becoming known in the west, especially by outlaws and ne'er-do-wells.

He walked across the street, his eyes always moving, watching everything, everyone, as if he were walking through Apache country. Spur moved like a cougar, smoothly, alert, ever ready to dart one way or the other to avoid or confront.

Low on his right hip rode a tied down, well worn holster that carried a long barreled Colt .45. He had been known to drive six penny nails with .45 slugs from that weapon from thirty yards.

Spur stepped up to the desk of the hotel, registered under the name of Colt Smith. He paid for his lodging with a ten dollar gold piece, asking for two nights. The fee was fifty cents a night.

"What floor ye want?" a wild eyed young man asked as he scratched a pimple on his neck.

"Second floor," Spur said.

"Fine, put ye in 204, that's center and looks down on the street. Ye a bounty hunter, mister?"

"Not so you could notice. Why, are you a wanted desperado?"

The kid laughed, gave Spur his key then sobered. "Truth of the matter, I am. Wanted in New York by my wife, but I ain't about to go back. She was as ugly as a box of rocks. Now her ugly wasn't just skin deep. No, sir. Her ugly went right down to the bone!"

Spur laughed, picked up his bag and walked up the stairs to 204. The room was like a thousand others he had stayed in. A square box with one window, thin curtains blowing in the afternoon breeze, a bed, a small dresser with a mirror that had wavy lines in it and with the silver peeling off the back. A washstand with a large crockery bowl and a pitcher filled with water. He was lucky. This room had a straight backed, wooden chair. It would come in handy for locking his door at night.

Spur looked down on the Greensburg street: dusty from two months without rain. Littered with horse droppings. A few merchants picked up the droppings every morning from in front of their stores after they swept the boardwalk. But not enough of them picked up the manure to do much good.

The main street was a block long each way, with only a few businesses on the side streets. On the far side he saw that houses crowded right up to the back of some of the stores with only an alley between them. Not exactly St. Louis or Chicago. Maybe a thousand people.

He pulled the wooden chair up to the window and sat down looking out. Somewhere out there could be a killer, one with a particular twist. He hated lawmen, any kind of lawmen, anywhere, at any time. How could he find a man like that?

He would see the sheriff and stay glued to him like a second skin until something happened—or until word came in of a lawman murdered by the same method in another town. Then the chase would begin again.

Spur nodded, affirming his moves. He had to stay ahead of the killer, be out front, ready to stop the crime and catch the murderer. Sure, easy to say. Now he had to get out on the street and do it.

2

Spur made sure his six-gun was loaded and ready. He eased it in and out of the holster twice to be sure it didn't hang up, then left his carpetbag on the bed and went out and locked his door.

He found the Sheriff's Office & Jail a block down along Main Street. Greensburg was a normal Western town. This one's main reason for being was cattle, a few coming through on trails, but most of them raised on the unending flat great plains that stretched interminably in every direction around Greensburg.

Spur pushed open the sheriff's door and saw that it was made of two-inch sturdy oak. A wise precaution. Eight feet ahead of the door, a counter went across the room with a narrow pass through. Behind the counter sat two men, one in his forties, one barely out of his teens.

"Sheriff in?" Spur asked. He saw the older man flinch, his hand went to a holstered gun on his left side. Then he stood and came to the counter.

"I'm Sheriff Bjelland. What can I do for you?"

"Colt Smith is my name, Sheriff. Wondered if we could talk privately?"

He held out his hand. "Possible, but I hold your six-gun while we talk."

"Good move, Sheriff Bjelland. More than glad to oblige." Spur gave him his hogleg and they went into the back where the four jail cells had been built solidly into the structure.

"You must have received the notice about lawmen getting killed between here and Wichita."

"I did and I've taken special precautions. Haven't been going around much alone anymore."

"Good idea. I'm here to try to catch the killer. You heard about Sheriff Wilson, I imagine."

"Known Clyde for twenty years." He looked up, curious. "You one of them Federal marshals or something?"

"Close enough. I'm going to be watching your backtrail for the next few days. Hope you don't mind."

Sheriff Bjelland squinted as he eyed Spur. "How do I know you're not the gent who's trying to kill me? You got a paper says who you be?"

"Do you carry a paper like that around, Sheriff? Something like that can get a man killed."

"Don't need to carry no paper. These folks hereabouts know me. I don't know you."

Spur reached in his shirt pocket and took out the telegram with his orders on it. He unfolded it and handed it to the lawman. The sheriff read the long telegram through.

"Never heard of this Capital Investigations. Who are they?"

"The Secret Service of the United States Government. We can't advertise who we are. You never can tell who is watching the telegraph office."

The sheriff folded the yellow paper and gave it back to Spur.

"Makes sense." He stuck out his hand. "Glad to meet you, whatever your real name is. And I'll be damn glad when this foolishness is all over."

"The four lawmen back the stage line don't think it's foolishness, they think of it as dead. Just be careful. I'll try to stay with you like a blanket. Do you check doors after dark?"

"Used to, guess I just decided not to. My deputy will do it tonight."

"You'll stay here the rest of the day, and tonight? Sleep here?"

"I'm a widower, nothing to go home for. Yes, I'll sleep in. You go look around, get acquainted with our town, try and spot your killer. I've only got two deputies. One is here now, I'll tell the other one about you when he comes on, so he don't drygulch you. He's a bit fast with a gun."

"Obliged." Spur took back his six-gun, pushed the long barreled weapon in his holster and went out the door. He walked the street from one end to the other on both sides. A few more stores than most places this size. That must mean there were a few ranchers and farmers out there who came to town now and then for supplies.

He went back to the hotel for supper. Just as he stepped into the lobby a woman came down the stairs. She wasn't a flashy "stopper" type that he had seen in Denver and St. Louis. Rather she had an understated kind of beauty and elegance that caught his eye. She was dressed in a pretty and he guessed expensive outfit that had a little jacket, and he saw earrings and a string of pearls around her neck.

She looked his way and their eyes met for a moment. She turned away and smiled softly as she walked into the hotel's small dining room.

He followed her in, saw her sitting at a table for two alone, and without a moment's hesitation walked to her table. "The place is terribly crowded tonight and I wondered if I might share your table?"

She looked up without surprise or fear as if she had guessed he might be coming over. She checked the dozen empty tables in the dining room and smiled.

"It is crowded. Won't you please sit down?"

He liked the soft voice, the easy way she had handled it. He was not sure what she would do.

He sat down and put his hat on the floor beside him.

"You must not be a cowboy, you don't eat supper with your hat on," she said. There was a touch of an accent but he couldn't tie it down.

"No, Miss. I don't. I grew up in New York. Oh, my name is Colt Smith." He used his cover name automatically.

"Colt, that does sound like a cowboy, or at least a weapons manufacturer. You're not that Colt?"

"No, afraid not."

"Just as well. My name is Lila Pemberthy. Are you new in town, too?"

"Yes, how did you know?"

"I saw you register earlier this afternoon."

They ordered their meals. The menu was easy to understand and limited. There was a choice of country stew or a steak dinner. She had a small portion of the stew and coffee. Spur ordered the biggest steak and all the side dishes. She watched him eat with amusement.

"You here on business?" she asked.

"Yes, Miss Pemberthy. Land. I represent a firm in Chicago and St. Louis that is interested in land speculation. My job is to find good land, cheap and buy it."

"That sounds interesting."

"Are you just traveling?"

"In a way. Actually I have a week's engagement to sing at the Bar None Saloon. Usually I sing in the opera house or some kind of hall. But there isn't any such thing here."

"A real entertainer! I'm honored to share your table. What time do you perform?"

"Three times, seven, nine and eleven. I've done the eastern cities and decided to come west for a change. My goodness, things certainly are different out here."

Spur smiled and cut up his steak. "Different isn't always pleasant. I hope you have some protection at that time of night when you leave the saloon."

She laughed softly. "Oh, yes, the barkeep arranges for an escort back to the hotel. It's only a block. It's quite safe really. I always carry a six-inch long hat pin. It can be a remarkably effective weapon."

They chatted about the weather and politics and the problems of travel, then she stood. He rose quickly.

"May I see you back to your room?" he asked.

"No, finish your supper. But my room number is 305, if you need to know."

Spur chuckled. "Was I that obvious?"

"Not quite. Will you come to hear me sing tonight?"

"If I can squeeze in the door. I bet the saloon will be jammed."

She nodded and left. Spur watched her walk away. She was interesting. He needed something to help him charge through this current assignment. How to find a killer when you don't even know for sure that he's in town, or that he's going to stop here?

He thought about it as he finished the steak, mashed potatoes and gravy, carrots, peas, pickled beets and three kinds of bread, butter and jam. The coffee was hot, plentiful and better than he usually found in hotels out here.

When the food was gone, he had decided if there was a better way to do the job, he couldn't think of it. He basically had to watch the town, watch the sheriff, look for strangers and anything unusual.

Then with a whole lot of luck, he just might stumble onto the killer before he could strike again.

That was the plan.

It wasn't a great plan but it was all he had.

Maybe Lila Pemberthy would help make the time go quicker as he waited. Maybe. On the other hand, she might be a totally proper lady who would not even let him past her hotel room door, and surely never see her trim ankle.

After supper, Spur toured the town again. Most of the retail stores were closed. He bought a box of .45 rounds at the hardware just as it was closing, then began to investigate the saloons.

There were seven in the small town. Four of them offered games of chance, everything from faro to poker, roulette, monte, Boston, seven up and euchre. Two had dance hall girls with dresses cut so low they left little to the imagination. The girls almost never danced. They spent most of their time flat on their backs, fucking up a storm in the two cribs upstairs.

The stairway up to the cribs were the most popular spots in town. Clients sat on the steps, waiting their turn. The only rule was that they had to have a beer or a whiskey in hand as they waited, or they forefeited their place in line.

Spur stayed in the last watering hole, the saloon that had a picture of Lila displayed on the door and again inside. It was the Bar None Saloon, and Lila was billed to sing at seven, nine and eleven, just as she had said.

He fell into his routine of playing some low stakes poker and listening to the saloon talk. In a strange town that was often the quickest way to get a feel for a place, learn what was going on and why it was happening.

A few of the men there had heard about the sheriff in the next town getting killed. None of them thought it could happen in Greensburg.

He won four dollars, then lost it again and quit fifty cents behind when Lila's first show came on.

The saloon was packed. All the poker table chairs were filled and thirty or forty men stood shoulder to shoulder behind them waiting for the songs.

There was no stage. A piano with two keys missing hunkered against the far wall. They had cleared back the poker tables for eight feet to give Lila some room near the piano. A piano player hit a few cords and the crowd cheered.

Lila walked out from the room behind the bar.

She was a looker.

Lila had a flare for theatrical makeup, yet she used only a little to highlight her natural beauty. The dress she wore cost more than the average cowboy's wages for three months, and it fit perfectly to show off her small but slender and well proportioned body, clinging delightfully.

Lila played it like a duchess, at least. She was a lady, and there was no need to announce it, or caution the men not to swear or use profanity. Lila was here!

She walked across the saloon to a hush, turned and nodded to the piano player and her voice wrapped around the sad song of "The Girl I Left Behind." It caught a lot of the men by surprise and there was a tear or two before she was done.

Lila moved out of that into "Jimmy Cracker," then "Old Dan Tucker," and plunged ahead into "My Love is Buried On The Wabash," a Civil War tear jerker.

When she paused at the end of the four songs the applause thundered amid whistles and stomping feet on the wooden floor.

Lila smiled at them as if they were children. She

was with them yet not really there, detached, unreachable, a memory/dream figment of the perfect woman of wonder that caught at them all. She was performing for them, yet alone, as if she were singing only for herself, or better, individually, for each man who heard her. Through it all her loneliness and her aloofness remained.

She sang again, roaring into "Garry Owen," the famous Seventh Cavalry battle song the troop used. This time she paused because the men knew where the ending was and they clapped and cheered and stomped.

She sang a dozen more songs. Many of the men remembered them from the East and the South. After every song the cheering raced through the crowd. More men crowded in from behind and gradually they pushed forward until she had only a small area to move around. She sang "The Bloody Monogahela" about the war and then "Rosie, You are My Posie." She closed with the haunting "Somewhere A Girl Waits For Me."

When the last song ended, the crowd waited in silence a moment, then burst into applause. The barkeep shouldered his way through the crowd, made a path for Lila and led her out of the saloon and into the back and small office where she had a tiny dressing room.

The men in the saloon cheered for five minutes, then the barkeep and owner shouted that Miss Lila would be singing again at nine and eleven, and the place settled down.

Spur went out and wandered the town, checking the other saloons, and soon spotted the sheriff making his rounds. He was checking doors and looking in at each of the saloons.

Spur waited for him to come away from the bakery door.

"Huh? Oh, you, Colt Smith. Yeah, I caved in. Figured I better earn my money. If that means some asshole shoots at me, I'll just shoot back. Got to be that way. Kind of the way I'm made, know what I mean, Smith?"

"I know. Figured it might happen. I'll be half a block behind you. Look sharp."

Nothing happened on the rest of the rounds.

They walked together from the next to last saloon to the Bar None.

"Usually stop in here last before I close up," Sheriff Bjelland said. "Mike's behind the bar. Known Mike since we both were kids in Missouri. You know there are over three hundred thousand souls living in St. Louis now? Christ, what a mob! Glad my folks got out of there when they did. Back in 1850 there weren't more than maybe seventy-five thousand."

They went into the Bar None. It was jammed. Lila was in the middle of her routine. It seemed to be the same songs in the same order for every show. Nobody minded. Most of them had never seen a lady sing this way before. They were mesmerized.

Spur found a spot against the wall near the piano and stood up. She noticed him at once and he thought there was a flicker of a smile between numbers. He was just wishing again. She was the picture of a lady, regal, proud, detached, desirable and totally unattainable.

DODGE CITY DOLL

Sheriff Bjelland slid behind the bar to talk to Mike. There was no place else to stand.

Lila closed with the same song she did the last time, "Somewhere a Girl Waits For Me." Again it had a shock effect on the men—a lot of them did have a girl somewhere waiting. Then, after a pause, the applause shook the place and they cheered for more.

Mike and Sheriff Bjelland made a path for Lila back to the office, and the customers drifted away, it being well past bedtime for the working men among them. A few cowboys had another beer before the long ride back to their spreads.

Mike came over to Spur and gave him a note. He opened it wondering what it said.

"Colt. Can you wait for me? I'd like you to see me back to our hotel . . . if you're not too busy buying land." It was a delicate feminine hand and could only be from Lila.

"Tell her, of course," Spur said, and Mike hurried through the rapidly emptying saloon.

When she came out, she had removed some of the makeup, but she still looked stunning. Her brown hair was piled on top of her head to make her look a little taller, he decided. She wore a soft brown sweater that matched her hair. He stood at the table he had taken when she walked up.

"Do you mind if we sit a minute? I always need to simmer down a little after I sing. It might not look like it, but I really work hard singing."

"I could see it. You don't just say the words, you seem to be feeling them. It could be emotionally draining."

She nodded. "That's the right words. I've never

figured it out quite that way before. I'd like a glass of white wine, but I don't want to drink it here. Would it . . ." She looked up at him for a moment then away. "No, I guess not. Forget the wine. I'm exhausted. Let's just walk back to the hotel. Performing never seems to get any easier."

She held his arm as they walked into the darkness. He could feel some nervous tension ebb from her.

"Oh, I hope you don't mind my grabbing your arm. I just feel safer this way. It isn't the darkness that is scary, it's all those men who looked at me while I was singing. Some of them thought I was their sweetheart. Some of them looked at me and remembered a mother, or a wife, or maybe a lover back east somewhere. It always happens. I . . . I just don't want to have to deal with them."

"I understand. I really don't mind your holding my arm. In fact I rather like it."

They went across the dusty street to the other side and down the boardwalk. The walks were always built by each store owner, covering the area in front of his store. Usually these walks were on the same level, but here and there, there were a few inches to step up or down.

At the hotel, they went up the broad steps to the first floor lobby and up to the second floor. They paused a moment, then went on to the third. He led her down to her room, 305, as he remembered.

"You have your key?" he asked.

She smiled. "Mr. Smith, I've been living in hotel rooms for the past three years. I've never lost a hotel key yet. And if I ever do, I have the three basic skeleton keys that open most door locks made today."

She smiled up at him and nodded. "Thank you for your escort service, Mr. Smith. Perhaps we'll see each other in the dining room again."

"Good night, Miss Pemberthy. I was delighted by your singing." Spur turned and walked toward the stairs. He paused there, saw her go in her room and close the door. He heard the faint click as she turned her lock.

McCoy checked off one good deed and went back to the street. He wanted to be sure that the sheriff was tucked safely in his office. That meant looking at the Bar None to see if he'd left and if he was checking doors again.

This was the third day since the death of the last lawman. The next attempt could come any time during the next four or five days. Spur shrugged. He didn't need all that much sleep anyway.

3

Spur spotted Sheriff Bjelland inside the Bar None Saloon and waited for him to come out. For the next hour, Spur tailed the lawman, never letting him know he was there, as Sheriff Bjelland checked store doors and hurried a few late drunks on their way home.

At last, a little after one in the morning, the sheriff went back to the jail, locked the door, leaving one deputy in charge of the night shift.

Spur walked a few doors down Main Street and sat in one of the chairs outside the bank. He tipped the chair back on its rear legs and watched the town. It slept. Most of the lights were out.

He tried to put himself in the killer's shoes. How would he do it? What kind of a ruse would he use to get the sheriff alone? Did he have a hatred for all lawmen, or just those in Kansas? What would motivate a man to do this random killing?

At the end of the half hour he gave up and went back to his hotel and crawled into bed. For a moment, he wondered if the beautiful lady in room

305 was asleep. He decided she was, blew out the lamp and settled down on the lumpy mattress.

McCoy did not see the songbird at breakfast. He had opened up the dining room at six-thirty. He ate three sunnyside up eggs over a stack of hotcakes and drank two cups of black coffee. His first check of the day was with the night deputy, still on duty at the jail.

Nothing had happened during the night; the sheriff was safe and sound, snoring in cell number one.

The next potential trouble spot Spur could figure: the stage was due in slightly after ten that morning.

Spur followed the sheriff to breakfast at the Johnson Cafe, saw him deliver two official documents, and hold a long discussion with the owner of the Mercantile, who was also the town's mayor.

The stagecoach was late when it pulled up in front of the freight depot with its four prancing horses. The flat landscape allowed only four instead of a team of six they had to use in the mountains.

The big Concord stage rolled in ten minutes late, but there had been no real problems, just a tired horse that wasn't exactly pulling her share.

Spur leaned against the Saddlery Shop as he watched the weary passengers get down from the Concord. Two men and a woman, and each seemed to be traveling alone. He checked the men critically.

One was a drummer of some kind, whose sample case never left his hand as he supervised the unloading of two heavy boxes from the boot.

The second man was a cowboy, with saddle, rifle

and small carpetbag. Neither of them looked like a loco killer hunting his fifth victim.

The trouble was, if you didn't know who the killer was, he could be almost anyone.

A young man hurried up to a woman who had arrived and hugged her tightly, then grabbed her valise. They chattered away as they walked down the boardwalk toward a buckboard. All accounted for.

Four passengers got on the stage. The horses had been changed in quick time. The two new teams were hitched and the driver made sure the passenger doors were closed. Then he cracked his big whip and the four horses strained ahead, got the heavy wagon moving again, then went faster and faster and raced out of town.

Spur grinned. It was company policy on most stage lines to charge quickly in and out of each town, giving the local population a show. Outside of town a ways the rig settled down to a steady pace once the show was over.

A pistol cracked through the sudden quietness after the departure of the stage. The shot came from down toward the sheriff's office. Spur leaped off the boardwalk and sprinted toward the sound.

Another shot boomed, a deeper sound, more like a .44 or a .45 caliber. A wagon passed out of the way and then Spur could see the sheriff's office. A man lay in the dust as the lawman kicked away a revolver. The man on the ground held his right arm which was already bathed in rich, red blood.

"Get me a doctor! I'm bleeding to death," the shot up man screamed.

"Too bad," Sheriff Bjelland said.

Spur rushed up and grabbed the weapon out of the dirt. It was too small for a .45. Looked like it could be one of the Remington New Line Revolver #3's, a .38 caliber.

Spur walked over to Sheriff Bjelland. "What kind of a coyote is this one?"

"Damned foolish one, Colt. I served some papers on him and he thought it was all my fault. His argument is with the bank, not me."

"So he can't be the one we're looking for. Especially not with that little .38 caliber pop gun."

Spur helped get the man to jail, where the local doctor came and bandaged up the arm.

Spur faded out of the jail. All the killings had taken place at night. No reason why the bush-whacker should change his tactics now. Which meant McCoy had himself some spare time. He walked down to the livery stable and rented a horse and saddle and rode out of town a mile or two.

He stopped near a bank near the creek and un-limbered his .45. Spur set up some small rocks on a boulder and did some target practice with his long barreled .45.

The ten-inch barrel made the weapon a little slower to draw, but it gave Spur what he tested to be seventy-five percent greater accuracy. He was willing to give up a few hundredths of a second for a killing shot. He set more small rocks on top of the boulder and got back forty yards and tried to hit them. His hit rate was too low.

Spur came up to thirty yards and nailed the rocks almost every time. With a shorter barrel he would need to be nearer twenty yards to get that kind of accuracy.

He rode back into town, turned in the rented nag and walked the town again.

Nothing.

Back at the hotel he lay down on his bed and concentrated on going to sleep. He would get a few hours now and be up most of the night. Darkness was the time the killer liked best, it seemed. Spur could do darkness.

All evening he trailed the sheriff, from one doorway to the next, to the saloons. Nowhere was there any contact, any secret messages, any tries by anyone to talk to the sheriff covertly.

This evening the sheriff went into the jail just before the late night show by Lila and when Spur came in he waved.

"You can relax, Colt. I'm staying inside the rest of the night. You can listen to Lila sing and then have a good night's sleep."

Spur did listen to Lila. He waited after the show and she came out and sat at his table.

"Thank God he isn't here," Lila said when she sat down. Her face showed a strain, her eyes not confident now at all, but frightened. She checked around the saloon again, then visibly tried to relax.

"I really need that glass of white wine tonight," she said. "If I can persuade you to walk me to the hotel, I might even let you have a glass yourself."

"My working day is over," Spur said and they headed out the door. She caught his arm again and held tightly. This time she looked around all during the walk. Spur kept watchful at the alley and at deep recessed doorways. His right hand hung close to his .45, but there was no problem. No one approached them and soon they were inside the hotel.

"Oh, I'm so glad to be here!" Her eyes sparkled and the fear had vanished. "If I remember right, I promised you a glass of white wine, and the only wine I know about is an almost full bottle in my room. Would you like to climb an extra flight?"

A short time later in her room she automatically locked the door and glanced at him. "I always lock the door as soon as I come in, long time habit. Don't think it means anything other than just locking the door."

She took the bottle of white wine off the dresser. It had been opened. She picked two wine glasses from the top drawer and held them up.

"Courtesy of the Bar None Saloon," she said and laughed. "I've more than earned them. I must be tripling business for him this week. I wonder how much he's taking in. I might just come right out and ask him tomorrow."

She poured the two glasses of wine and smiled.

"Now it's time for you to tell me about yourself. Start by telling me where you grew up."

McCoy sipped the wine, it was good. "I was born in New York city and grew up there. My father runs some businesses and I worked for him for awhile after school."

"I bet you went to college, didn't you?"

"Yes, Harvard."

"And you graduated?"

"Yes, a few years ago. Business courses mostly."

"But you didn't like Daddy's kind of life, so you moved west and went into land speculation?"

"Close enough."

"Then what happened? Were you in the war?"

Spur told her about the war, his two years of fighting and then how he was called to Washington.

"Tell me about the parties. Do they have wonderful parties in Washington? Were the ladies all beautifully dressed and the men in their black ties and so handsome?"

"Yes, there were parties. I never went to many, I was busy working for the senator. He went to the parties. But I did get to a few. Yes, the women wore expensive gowns and it was all very exciting."

"I sang at a party once in Washington," she said. "It was kind of fancy. But then I had to leave to catch a train. I just love to ride on the trains, don't you, Mr. Smith?"

Spur said he enjoyed travel by train. Lila tipped her wine glass up and emptied it, then poured another one. She rubbed her wrist over her brow which was showing some signs of perspiration. A moment later she unbuttoned four of the buttons that held the dress tightly under her chin.

"And I bet you make a lot of money in land speculation, Colt Smith." She frowned, drank from the second glass of wine. "Smith? Are you sure that's your right name? Lots of people use that when they don't want anyone to know their real name."

She sat on the bed and unbuttoned two more fasteners on the top of her dress. Something lacy showed through. Lila didn't seem to notice.

She turned toward him where he sat next to her on

the bed. Her room had no chair. He saw the sway and bounce of her breasts under the chemise. She didn't notice.

"Tell me about New York. I've never been to New York. Is it as big as everyone says?"

"Yes, it has almost a million people. It's the biggest city in the whole nation. But it's still made up of a lot of small communities. Different nationalities seem to gather in one place."

She blinked at him, yawned and emptied her wine glass.

"I really love this white wine." She filled her glass again.

"Now, Lila, I've told you about me. You tell me about Lila Pemberthy. Where were you born?"

She smiled, drained the glass of wine and hiccuped. "Pardon me, I love wine." She poured a fourth glass and watched him. "Me, where was I born? Lousiana. Down there outside of New Orleans a ways. I went to school and everything." She sipped on the wine.

"You might think I'm getting tipsy from strong drink." She giggled. "Not so. I am fortifying myself from the cold night air. Right, from the cold, cold night air. And . . . and . . . and because I have to sleep alone. I used to be married. Did I tell you that? The best part of being married is to have somebody to warm your feet on. Did you know that?"

"I've never been married," Spur said.

She blinked. Most of the aloofness was gone, the regal bearing had slumped into her wine glass, and now she unbuttoned the rest of her dress front down to the waist. It was as though he wasn't there, or that he was her husband or another woman.

It seemed to make no difference that he was sitting beside her on the edge of the bed, and that they were alone in her hotel room with the door locked. Her dress fell away on one side and showed a finely sewn lace chemise that covered her breasts but revealed a soft white wrapper under the chemise.

Spur stood. "Thanks for the wine. It looks like it's about time for me to go."

"I want to talk some more. Don't go." Her eyes pleaded with him. "I don't get to talk to nice men very often. Usually the men I meet don't want to talk. You talk nice." She stood and lifted the dress off over her head and tossed it on the bed.

"Getting too warm in here. Are you warm?" Without waiting for an answer she poured another glass of wine. She sat on the side of the bed, totally at ease. Now she wore her shoes and long stockings that vanished under knee length drawers that showed under a flounce of three petticoats from her waist down. The lace chemise was the most beautiful Spur had ever seen.

Lila wasn't aware that she was half undressed. The wine must have done it, Spur decided.

"Really, it's time I was going."

Her face slid into a sly little smile. "If I kiss you, will you talk some more?"

"No, then I'd have to leave right away." He caught her hands when she moved toward him on the edge of the bed. "Lila, it isn't that I don't appreciate a beautiful girl. And you're one of the most beautiful I've ever seen. But I do have rules about taking advantage of a lady when she's had too much to drink. You have had too much to drink."

"Not so, not so, not so. There, I said it twice. Just relaxing after a long hard day of work in the saloon." She giggled again. "Mama would lift my skirts and paddle me good she see me now. With a *man* in my room!"

She laughed softly. "Speaking of working in the saloon. Do you know those two girls who work there really don't sell drinks? They go upstairs with men and . . . and do it . . . and get paid for it! I've never known a woman who *did it for pay*. Now that is just terrible. Fallen women. They are sure as hell, fallen women."

She pushed closer to him, put her arms around his neck and pulled his face toward hers. Her lips were warm and inviting against his as she kissed him. He edged away and unlaced her hands from his neck.

Spur leaned back and when she opened her eyes, he caught her attention. "Lila do you realize that you have taken your dress off?"

"No, no, no. I just was a little warm." She looked down, saw her petticoat and chemise and laughed. "I'll be damned. I'm half undressed." She giggled again and fell backward on the bed.

A moment later, she giggled again, then gave a long sigh and went to sleep. Spur smiled and rolled her over to get the covers down, then arranged her under the light quilt and sheet and snuggled the covers up to her chin.

"You're going to have a headache in the morning," he told her, as he slipped out of the room. He used her key and locked the door from the outside, then took out the key and pushed it under the door and went down to his room.

Morning came much earlier than Spur was ready for it. He was out of bed with the sun and waited for the dining room to open at six-thirty. He had shaved closely, trimmed his sideburns and moustache, combed his hair and had a whore's bath in the cold water from the pitcher.

He felt ready to take on the world, but not before breakfast.

That daily ritual out of the way, Spur settled his low crowned, brown Stetson on his head and ambled out the front door of the hotel. He was halfway to the sheriff's office when he turned quickly away from the street and pretended to stare in the first window he found, the hardware store. He looked over his shoulder as a pair of riders passed close to his side of the dusty street. For a moment he couldn't believe it.

The two dusty and trail weary men riding into Greensburg were two of the most wanted bank robbers in the west: Tex Rogers, and "Little Boy" Harry Marcello. There could be only one reason they were in town. They were here to rob the Greensburg State Bank.

4

McCoy watched the two riders moving down the street. Both looked bone weary. They pulled up to the hitching rail in front of the Lucky Chip Saloon, next to the other hotel and slowly eased out of their saddles.

They must have been riding a long time. One man took his saddlebags and they both banged on the saloon door. It wasn't open yet. They stood there a moment talking, then went into the hotel.

Spur walked past the hotel to the jail and found the sheriff having breakfast off a tray.

"Glad to see you looking so healthy, Sheriff Bjelland," Spur said, dropping into a chair beside the desk.

"Not half as happy as I am to be alive another day. Could you use some coffee?"

"Thanks, just ate. We've got some famous company in town. They just rode in. You've heard of them, Tex Rogers and 'Little Boy' Harry Marcello."

"Bankers, both of them!" the sheriff said, hardly missing a bite of the bacon, eggs and hashbrowns on his plate. "Them polecats team up and got only one project in mind and I don't like the idea attal."

"True, you best let the bank owner in town know what's happening. Rogers used to work with a gang of four. I didn't see anybody else who trailed them into town, and I been watching them for some time."

Bjelland's long face took on a toughness Spur was glad to see. "We had a bank man in town three four years ago. Nailed the son-of-a-bitch with a fifty-two caliber slug in his gut just as he stepped out of the bank with the loot. But he worked alone, at least that time."

"You could ask the bank to stay closed today, death in the family, maybe," Spur suggested.

"Can't. Merchants need change and want to make deposits. That's the only vault or safe we got in the whole town."

"I'll be glad to help," Spur said. "Can you get together six or eight men who know how to shoot straight? We'll set up a little reception committee for the banker specialists."

"Yep." The sheriff went to the front window and looked out. The bank was across the street and down half a block.

"Put a pair of riflemen across the way on top of the buildings," Spur suggested. "Maybe three to cover the front door of the bank. Does it have a back entrance?"

"Nope. Jesse built it that way so he'd just have one door to worry about. And it's brick, the only brick building in town. Can't burn it down."

"You get your posse, I'm going to find a chair

where I can watch the hotel and their horses. They didn't put the nags into the livery, so they must not plan on staying long. Probably not more than a few hours.''

Spur checked the .45 at his hip, went down to the hardware and looked for a rifle. The store man had three, and Spur picked the Winchester 1866 model. It was an improvement on the basic Henry repeating rifle the North used so effectively during the big war.

It weighed a little over nine pounds, was 43 inches long with a 24-inch octagon barrel with six grooves. The best feature was a tubular magazine under the barrel that held twelve .44 rim fire rounds. It would shoot thirteen times as fast as you could work the lever. The Rebels used to say the Northerners loaded the Henry on Sunday and fired all week without reloading.

He bought the rifle for thirteen dollars and fifty cents, a little overpriced, but he needed it. Rim fire rounds were fifty-seven cents for a box of fifty. He took two boxes and slid them in his pockets.

Spur stopped at the front door and pushed one round into the chamber, and loaded the long magazine with twelve more. Then he left the store and found a spot to sit in the sun where he could watch the dusty, sweat streaked horses in front of the other hotel. Spur set the rifle behind him, out of sight and eased his Stetson down over his face so he could barely see out. He could have a long wait.

The bank opened at ten, right on schedule. Spur hoped that the sheriff had told only the bank owner or manager about the threat. No sense creating a panic.

A half hour after he sat down, Spur checked the roof lines of the false fronts behind him. He saw movement in two spots and as he watched closer, he could see a man changing positions where he sat in the shadows. Two men up, Spur just hoped they were from the sheriff and not a part of the robber gang.

Twenty minutes later Spur stood to stretch, just as the two robbers came out of the hotel. Both were picking their teeth. So it had been food they were after, not a bath or a bed. The two men checked their horses, tightened the saddle cinches which had been loosened and led their mounts down the street. They tied them at a hitching post down the alley next to the bank.

Then they sat in chairs in front of the bank and waited.

As Spur watched the street, he realized there weren't as many people moving around as usual. Only half a dozen rigs were parked on the block where the bank was. Now and then someone left a store, but it was usually to go a short distance to another store.

A rider came into town. His horse looked trail weary. The man wore two pistols and had a rifle in his saddle boot. He reined in across from the bank and fiddled with his horse and saddle.

The man was on the same side of the street as Spur was and he had trouble keeping an eye on him. A few minutes later, two more men rode in at a walk, also tied up on Spur's side of the street across from the bank. They were in no rush to leave their mounts. Both had pistols and Spur spotted rifles in their boots.

Now there was no one on the street. Spur couldn't see the sheriff's office from where he was. Rogers and Marcello lounged near the front of the bank, then stood and wandered into the front door of the money lender.

The men on his side of the street pulled out their rifles and spent a lot of time checking them and their saddles. They were stalling, staying in position ready to defend the robbers when they burst out of the bank.

There was a tension in the air. He was sure the men could feel it. They had to know something was wrong. Nobody moved on the street. Usually there would be half a dozen buggies and wagons driving up and down the dusty avenue and twenty or thirty townsfolk and ranchers walking around.

Spur had checked his pocket watch. The pair was in the bank for five minutes, then he heard a muffled shot. A moment later both men charged out of the bank. Rogers, the taller one, held a woman in front of him.

Spur dove to the boardwalk, lifted the Winchester and fired before the unprotected man could make a break for his horse. The heavy .44 slug caught Marcello in the shoulder and spun him around. He stumbled and fell, dropping a large canvas bag. He lifted his gun and fired wildly. Spur put a second round into his chest and he flopped over and lay still.

One of the robber gang on Spur's side of the street turned and snapped a pistol shot at Spur. McCoy returned fire, missed as the robber dove to the ground. But Spur's second shot caught the robber in the side of the head and silenced him forever.

In the few seconds Spur defended himself, Rogers had hoisted the small woman under one arm, sprinted to his horse and climbed on board.

Down the street Spur saw the sheriff and two deputies charge toward the horseman. A rifle barked from the rooftops and nicked Rogers' horse as he charged down the alley away from the guns. Another rifle snarled and Sheriff Bjelland went down with a bullet in his leg.

One of the horsemen on Spur's side of the street leaped aboard his mount and charged for the alley. Six shots barked and the horse and rider went down. The rider rolled and tried to run but the rooftop rifle cut him down.

A horse galloped down the other alley and suddenly the street was silent.

The doctor ran out to tend to Sheriff Bjelland. Spur checked the two riders who had been giving covering fire for the robbers. Both were dead. The bandit's horse in the middle of the street had to be put out of its misery.

In front of the bank Spur knelt by Marcello. He would never rob another bank again. Under his body was a sack filled with paper money, much of it stained with the robber's blood.

Spur ran over to the sheriff.

The bank owner was already there.

"He took Mindy Lou!" the man screamed. "We've got to get a posse to go after him. He kidnapped my Mindy Lou!"

Sheriff Bjelland winced and then yelped in pain when the doctor tried to rip down his pants leg. The doctor let Bjelland sit easy for a minute, then he held his toe and pulled it outward.

"That feel better?"

"Lordy, yes."

"Sheriff, you can't take a posse anywhere. You have a bad wound."

"My deputies will lead the posse," Bjelland said through his pain. "Get them moving. You go, too, Smith. They'll need you. Get at least ten men."

Five minutes later twelve men rode out of town following the trail of the robber with his captive. Spur took the lead and found the trail, then followed it down the main road toward Wichita.

A half mile out of town the robber angled toward a small farm. He rode through the place without even stopping, but the maneuver cost the posse almost an hour as they approached the buildings cautiously. At last the farmer came out of the barn and waved at them.

"Yeah, saw a man come through here. Seemed to have somebody with him who didn't want to go, some young woman."

Spur thanked him and they charged out east on a trail that they found was parallel with the main road.

Spur rode a borrowed horse, cradled the Winchester over his saddle and watched the ground. Rogers was making no attempt to hide his trail. Even if they caught up with him, he had the hostage and could force them to hold back. They couldn't fire at him for fear of hitting the girl.

Spur looked at the posse. Two deputy sheriffs who were young and seemed inexperienced, two merchants who appeared competent, a trio of cowboys just off the range, and three townspeople who Spur knew nothing about. All but two had rifles.

Gradually the trail led back to the main road to Wichita. Rogers must have decided not to take a chance riding into a gopher hole and snapping his mount's leg. The road would be safest, and quickest.

When they hit the road again, Spur speeded his tracking. He would ride at a gallop for a quarter of a mile, get off his horse and check the trail carefully until he found the double loaded hoofprints of Roger's horse, then he mounted again and rode flat out for another quarter mile. The main group of the posse cantered along behind keeping up with him.

At noon the two cowboys wanted to stop to make coffee. Nobody had any coffee or any food. When the cowboys discovered that, they turned around and without a word rode back toward town.

About one o'clock they stopped at a small rise. Spur knew they were gaining on the outlaw. Rogers' horse was tired when it started. Unless he found a new mount, they should have him in their sights within another two hours.

Rogers had a choice. He could drop off the girl and make better time, or he could keep the girl and use her life as a bargaining chip. Spur figured Rogers would keep the girl. It gave him his best chance. Rogers had lived through a dozen scrapes like this. He would know the odds.

He kept the girl.

At three that afternoon, they were within rifle

range of the pair but didn't dare shoot. Spur told the others to stay behind and he rode hard, circled around and came out in front of the outlaw. He dragged a stack of dead brush into the stage coach road at a narrow place through a woods where Rogers would either have to slow down to force his way through the dead branches, or ride around it into the woods.

Spur was ready behind a big cottonwood tree when Rogers rode up. He swore and slowed. Spur aimed carefully with the Winchester. The girl sat astride behind Rogers, her arms locked around his chest, her skirt riding up to her waist.

At this angle McCoy could hit Rogers without endangering the girl. Spur refined his aim. Rogers stopped for a moment.

Spur fired.

The round hit Rogers in the left shoulder, away from the girl. He nearly fell off the horse but held on. He grabbed the girl with his good right hand to keep her on board, and crashed through the brush with his mount and pounded down the road.

"I'll kill her if you try to shoot at me again!" Rogers bellowed as he rode away.

Spur met the posse at the brush as he was clearing it away. No sense making the stage stop here. It could look like a robbery attempt on the big Concord.

"What the hell happened?" Turner, the lead deputy, asked.

Spur told them. "He's wounded. So he won't be moving far before he stops to take care of that shoulder. He warned us about shooting again or he would kill the girl. He won't. Then he wouldn't have any protection."

"So what the hell can we do?" one of the merchants asked.

"We wait and follow him. He's got to sleep sometime, sleep and eat and guard the girl. He can't do everything."

"He'll tie up the girl," the other cowboy said.

"Probably, but he still has to sleep. If he makes a fire we'll find him easily by the smell of the smoke. We'll keep going and track him. Those shoe prints are easy to find with him riding double.

"If we have a chance to shoot at him again, it's got to be a killing shot."

They rode.

It was nearly four that afternoon when they saw him again. The land had flattened out ahead as they came over a small rise. Down trail they spotted the yellow dress the girl wore. She stood beside the horse less than half a mile ahead.

Rogers pulled her aboard and they vanished in a blush of small trees and brush beside a creek.

When it grew dusk, Spur stopped the posse and brought them together.

"He has two choices. He can keep on moving and risk passing out and falling off his mount. Or he can stop and tie up the girl and try to get some rest and hope we don't find him. My guess is that he'll move maybe half a mile off the trail, make a fire, fix himself some coffee and maybe some beans. His mount was outfitted for the trail when he came in this morning, so he still has a grub sack."

"So how can we find him in the dark?" a towner asked.

"We move ahead until I can't make out the tracks anymore, then we spread out in a company front about fifty yards apart. It gives us a long line a quarter of a mile on each side of the trail. If he makes a fire tonight, one of us is going to smell it. When you spot him, get everybody together and we'll decide what to do."

Turner, the lead deputy agreed. "Yeah, let's do it. This gent has been on this kind of hunt before. None of the rest of us have, so we do it his way."

They spread out. Spur took the farthest position on the right side of the road. He was guessing. Most men were right handed. He figured Rogers would turn right when he wanted to find some cover. Along here the trail was on the left side of the stream.

They moved ahead at a walk, tried to keep in sight of one another, but Spur knew that would not happen. There was no moon as it got dark, and you could see only about fifty feet in any direction.

They covered a mile, maybe a mile and a half, and Spur wondered if he had guessed wrong.

Another half mile and he figured he had. He was riding up a small rise, with the stream well below and to the left. An owl hooted somewhere to his right. It was real, no Indians were left around in Kansas.

They moved through the countryside for a half hour. Now and then he heard or saw the man next to him toward the road. They rode and watched, sat and listened. Always they sniffed the clean, pure air for the taint of wood smoke.

For another fifteen minutes he saw nothing ahead but blackness. Then the slight breeze stirred and brought to him the thin, unmistakable smell of smoke.

Where?

He rode forward and the smoke was stronger. He rode, angled to the left and it decreased. He changed to the right and forward and lost it all together.

Spur backtracked and moved toward the stream. The smoke came to him again and this time he followed it upwind. He got off his mount, took the Winchester and moved slowly through the slightly downhill prairie.

He wondered if it were a rancher's cabin, or a sodbuster. They hadn't seen any habitation out this way for miles.

Ahead there was a clump of brush. Now he could see the soft glow of light. The fire!

Spur edged closer, moving like an Apache withut rustling a leaf, without breaking a twig. When he was twenty yards away he saw someone move.

Closer, he had to get closer. The brush here prevented any kind of sure shot.

He worked up slowly, not wanting to risk Rogers using his gun on the girl. No sense in that. Slow and easy. He had all night.

After another ten minutes he had moved around the pair to where there was almost no brush. He could see them now in the soft glow of the small cooking fire. The girl did not seem to be tied up.

He heard them talking, both softly. He must have warned her not to make any noise. Then he smelled the coffee, and the crisp, sharp odor of frying bacon. Rogers must be confident.

Spur angled closer, crawling on hands and knees

now until he was ten yards away. The girl must have been lying down. Now she lifted up and in the light of the fire he saw that she wore nothing above her waist. Her firm, young breasts swung out and bounced and jiggled as she moved. Mindy Lou did not look at all like a hostage. She smiled and held out both arms.

"Darling! It's been so long. I didn't think you were ever coming to get me out of that stuffy old bank. Let's make it just as good as we did the other time. I'm sure those men have gone home. We haven't heard anything from them. I've got your shoulder all bandaged up and the beans aren't ready yet. We can do a quick one now and then take our time on the next four or five."

Tex Rogers laughed delightedly and turned toward her.

"You're right, Mindy Lou, it's been too damned long."

5

The two bare bodies stretched out on the blanket in
the faint firelight and Spur worked closer. There
could be no mistakes. He wanted them dead to
rights if either tried to pull a pistol off the blanket.

A minute later the pair coupled on the blanket
were groaning and laughing and yelping with
delight when Spur saw a visitor. He saw the twin
coals of fire in the eyes of the animal first. Then as it
crept closer on its belly, he knew what it was. A
coyote, a rabid coyote or it never would get this
close to humans.

Being rabid it was also half starved and would
take on any prey it could find, even man. One bite
from those saliva drooling teeth and the human
would suffer a sure and painful death from rabies.

Spur moved his Winchester's muzzle to the left to
cover the animal, saw it creep three feet closer to the
couple and spring. Spur's follow shot caught the
thin coyote as it hurtled through the air. The heavy
slug cut a swath through its chest and heart and

tore out through the other side of the coyote.

The report of the rifle brought a scream from Mindy Lou, a string of curses from Tex Rogers, and a new scream as the coyote landed at the very edge of the blanket.

Mindy Lou sat up, not trying to hide her breasts as she screamed again and again and stared at the dying coyote.

"Don't either of you move!" Spur bellowed. "You're both under arrest."

Spur did not show himself. Rogers had dropped out of sight and Spur was sure he was crawling for his guns.

"Come on, Rogers, give it up or you're dead."

Only silence answered him.

Mindy Lou finished screaming and edged away from the dead coyote. Then in a flurry of action, a six-gun cracked twice and Spur saw a figure wearing only pants and boots, leap up and scramble deeper into the brush and toward a big cottonwood. Spur snapped one shot at the darting figure, but he figured he missed.

"No way out, Rogers. We've got this camp surrounded and covered with ten guns. You saw us following you."

"Not a chance, asshole!" Rogers called from behind the cottonwood. "You stumbled on us and we got lucky with that damn coyote. Be a hero, rescue the girl. You'll never find me moving alone in the dark."

Spur fired the Winchester at the voice three times. It would act as a signal to the rest of the posse to join him here. He also might wing Rogers.

Then the night quieted. The girl rustled around, putting on her clothes. Spur listened but could hear no movement from Rogers.

Horse? Where had Rogers tied up his horse? Spur lifted up and moved through the brush with no attempt to be quiet. He circled the little camp and found nothing. He made a wider circle and reached a tributary to a small stream with the main trail to Wichita followed. He heard a horse snorting. He crashed that way only to hear saddle leather creak, and to see the backside of the bay charging into the darkness to the east.

Spur sent three shots after the rider, then walked back to the campfire and found Mindy Lou fully dressed sitting beside the blaze. She looked up at him, her dark eyes angry. She held a pistol that now pointed at him.

"This six-gun is for my protection and I know how to use it," she said simply.

"Doesn't look like your virtue needs much protection, Mindy Lou."

She lowered the weapon and pouted. He figured she was not more than eighteen.

"Just don't tell my uncle. He'd just die. Truth is, I've known Tex for two years. He came to town to rob the bank back then and I talked him out of it. We went to bed instead. He's been back every few months. But this time he said he needed the bank's money and this would be an ideal time for him to take me with him. He's been the only one. I've been in love with him since the first time I saw him."

Spur sat there watching her. Her hands fiddled with her dress, fed small sticks into the fire. She glanced up at him from time to time, her face softening.

"Miss, I'd say any problems you have with your uncle are your own business. Won't do any good for me to tell him about your little roll in the blankets out here." He stood. "Build up the fire, I've got a posse to find."

He fired three more shots, then called into the Kansas night, and after a half hour he had all but one of the posse in the fold.

"All right men. We nearly had Tex, but he got lucky and slipped away. Mindy Lou here is safe, and come dawn, I want most of you to head back to Greensburg and take her along. Missy Mindy Lou is your charge and I expect you to treat her like a lady. Anybody who doesn't will be reported to the sheriff."

He looked at them in the firelight. "Which one of you is the best shot?"

The cowboy spoke up when no one else did. "I've used a weapon now and then. Did three years as a sniper with the 27th Michigan Volunteers in the war."

"Fine, what's your name?"

"Froude, sir. Ken Froude."

"I'd like to take you with me now, tonight, to track Rogers. Are you volunteering?"

Froude grinned. "Sir, you know the rule, never volunteer for anything. Yeah, I'm with you."

Spur nodded. "The rest of you get some sleep and ride back to Greensburg in the morning. Might post a guard if you want, mostly to watch for rabid coyotes. Where there's one, there's bound to be others."

Ten minutes later Spur and Froude checked the main stage road toward Wichita. Spur found enough dry grass to twist into a torch and work back and forth across the road. He spotted the same looking horseshoe mark he had been tracking before. It was more square than most of the shoes in use. This mark had no insect tracks over it as most of the others did. No nighttime bug had crawled over this one, so it must have been made within the past hour or so.

"This has to be the one," Spur said. "Let's ride a half mile and check again."

The second time they made a torch and checked. They could not find the tracks.

"He's holed up somewhere waiting for morning. The girl told me his shoulder is hit pretty bad. He can't put his weight on it, and he didn't unsaddle his horse because he didn't think he could throw the saddle on come morning."

Spur looked into the blackness, and listened for any night birds. He could always go back for more men. He made his tactical decision the way he used to in the Army.

"Froude, I want you to lay low here until morning. If I flush him out, he'll come this way. If he does, pretend you're back in the Army and blast him out of the saddle. He's wanted for murder and bank robbery. You'll be doing the country a favor."

"Yeah, I can do that. You think he'll run?"

"First I have to find him. He won't make another fire, that's for damned sure. If nothing happens by noon, and you don't hear any shots, take off for town."

"I'll come hunting you, Smith."

"Might be too late. This is going to be one on one."

Spur turned and rode back down the stage trail for two hundred yards, made another torch and searched for the prints. Nothing. He repeated the procedure twice more before he found the hoofprints he wanted. They led on down the road for another fifty yards, then turned off into the trees along the small stream.

Spur stamped out the torch and jumped to one side, but there was no barrage of hot lead from the brush. If Rogers saw the torch he kept hidden, figuring he could stay out of sight until he and his horse were rested.

McCoy was counting on Rogers' horse to give away his hiding spot. If Rogers was down and sleeping, he wouldn't be able to hold his mount.

A horse has a fine sense of smell, and can sense another horse up to a quarter of a mile if the wind is right. The animals are curious and usually will whinny or wicker or make some other sound in communication. Mares talk a lot more than the stallions.

Spur hoped Tex's mount was feeling friendly and ready for some horse talk. He marked the trail where the tracks vanished, then rode slowly fifty yards each way listening carefully, but heard no contact.

Back at the mark he rode into the brush, which was only about twenty yards wide on both sides of the creek. He splashed through the water and walked his mount out the other side, then sat and listened.

Nothing.

He rode fifty yards up and back on the far side of the creek, but had no response. McCoy penetrated the brush at several points, but his mount did not respond. The other horse might be so worn out it was sleeping on its feet. Or Tex might have tied a bandanna around its muzzle so it couldn't make any sounds. Spur hoped that wasn't the case.

The Secret Agent moved into the brush every ten yards now, probing, examining, determined to find Rogers before he could run again. If he got on his horse and rode, this could turn into a two week chase. Spur didn't have time for that. This was a side trip. He was hunting a lawman killer.

On the sixth invasion of the brush from the far end, he paused again. This time he heard a snort and some horse talk. It came from dead ahead, not more than another ten yards. Spur slid off his mount, left the Winchester in the boot and worked ahead through the light brush and small willow and cottonwoods with all the stealth of a Chiricahua Apache.

He never put his weight on his foot until he was sure there was no branch or twig under it. No tree was scraped or green bough rustled. It took him five minutes to cover five yards. When he edged around the last thicket he saw the horse in the darkness. It was tied to a sapling on a grazing line and munching away on the spring grass.

Spur checked the surrounding area he could see without moving. Nowhere did he spot a blanket roll. He eased up to the horse, smoothed its flank, rubbed its neck, then untied the animal and led it downstream and, he hoped, away from the bank robber.

Ten minutes later, both horses were tied and hidden. He returned to the same spot and began searching for Tex. It was a grinding, slow, monotonous job. It was too dark to see his pocket watch. The trees and clouds hid the Big Dipper so he couldn't judge the time by that.

McCoy kept searching. He made two circles around the place where Tex's horse had been without finding him. Tex couldn't be more than twenty or thirty yards away. He had to be here somewhere.

He moved forward and a bramble bush raked his wrist bringing blood. He stopped.

Yeah! Slowly he moved around the six-foot high, twenty feet in diameter, impenetrable mound of thick growth with thorns on it that would make a rosebush blush with shame. He remembered that the bramble bushes were the favorite hiding spots for Indians on the run. They worked around the brushy bush until they found an opening at the bottom, and wormed their way in underneath, safely below the mass of thorns and thickets.

He had to go around the brambles twice before he found the right spot. There were no brambles to the ground and a small opening showed. He knelt at it and felt the ground. It had been disturbed. He found indentations and scrapes that could have been made by boots as someone crawled forward.

Spur moved back ten yards, found a good sized cottonwood and settled down. He had a perfect shot at the entrance and when Tex came crawling out, he would be in no position to defend himself.

Spur turned his back to the bramble bush, opened

the light jacket he wore and lit a match to check the time. Two-thirty A.M. He had a long wait ahead of him.

He dozed, then gave himself a wake up call at four-thirty and went to sleep. He woke promptly and checked the time with another match. Twenty-eight after four. Good.

He slid a sixth round into his .45 and hunkered down watching the bramble bush.

With the first streaks of dawn tingeing the east, Spur slid to a prone position to offer a smaller target and watched the bramble opening. Coyotes could have used the brambles as a den. If so, there should be plenty of room inside where the animals would have chewed off the dead branches so they could move around. Spur had seen one bramble bush that had a space four feet high inside. Some children at a small ranch had shown the bush to him one day. They had used clippers and cut out some of the dead wood and live shoots inside to make a playhouse.

Just as dawn came, and the light gave him a full view of the bramble bush, Spur was glad he had not tried to crawl in. The opening looked smaller now, less than a foot off the ground, but room enough to slip in.

Ten minutes later he heard someone cough. The sound came from the brambles.

Another five minutes went by before Spur saw movement at the opening. Tex Rogers crawled forward slowly, seemingly in pain. He let his left arm drag behind him, pulling himself outward with his right elbow digging in the dirt. Spur could tell that the man was hurting.

Spur hurried to one side before Tex could see and when the killer was half-way out, Spur planted his heavy boot on Tex's neck and pushed down.

"What the hell?"

"Morning, Tex. Have a good night's sleep?"

"Bastard!"

Spur moved his foot. "Come on out, but remember, I won't need more than a small excuse to put a slug right between your eyes. That would get my day off to a fine start."

Once Tex was out of the brambles, Spur stripped the .44 from his holster, took a hideout derringer from his pocket and two knives from his ankle.

His shoulder had a bandage of sorts around it made from cloth from a petticoat.

"You'll live until you hang," Spur said pushing him forward toward the spot where he had hidden the horses.

Back on the road, Spur tied Tex's hand in front of him and held the reins to his horse. Spur fired three times in the air, and a few minutes later, Ken Froude rode up, his rifle ready, his dark eyes curious.

"Damn, you got the bastard," he said.

"Yeah, and the only place he's going is to a hangman's trap. He's wanted in at least three states for bank robbery and murder."

They rode into town just before noon. Word spread quickly and before they got to the jail, half the town was in the street to see the killer. He wasn't much to look at, still dirty, bearded and with stringy, dirty hair.

One of the deputies who had been on the posse met them in front of the jail.

"Mr. Smith, I think you better come inside," the deputy said.

"Trouble?" Spur asked.

Inside Spur looked around. "Where's Sheriff Bjelland?" Spur asked.

"That's what I wanted to talk about. The sheriff is dead. Somebody shot him last night while we were gone. Gunned him down at the edge of town."

Spur's face tightened into a scowl. "He was killed with two .45 rounds, fired so close there were powder burns, right? And he was killed at night and there are no witnesses."

"Yeah, but how could you know all that?"

"Throw this bank robber in a cell, I want to see the sheriff's body!" Spur spat and rushed out the door. He had been here two days and now this happened the minute he was out of town. There had to be a tie in. Did the repetitive killer know that Spur was after him? Or was this all a coincidence? Spur McCoy was damned well going to find out!

6

McCoy knew he was right before he looked at the cold, waxy body of ex-sheriff Jon Bjelland. The first bluish hole with a ring of powder burn marks around it was a little lower than he might have guessed, but it did the job. It disabled the sheriff and made the second shot easy.

He wondered if this killing bastard talked to his victims during the time between the two slugs. Did he let the man last for an hour, sweating and screaming in pain? Did he make the sheriff listen to a diatribe about how terrible lawmen were and that they all should be shot once in the belly so they had to suffer for an hour before they died?

Spur slammed his hand against the table on which Bjelland lay in the back room of the barber shop. The barber was also the undertaker and the official county coroner. What churned in Spur's gut was the fact that Bjelland wouldn't be dead if Tex Rogers hadn't come to town.

One of the deputies said the sheriff must have been out rattling doors on the night shift and somebody got to him. Yeah, somebody, but who, and how, and when, and most importantly, why?

Spur pulled the sheet back over the body.

"I got to dress him up nice," Dorian, the barber-undertaker said. "Folks expect to see a body dressed nice."

"You do that!" Spur snarled. "All I have to do is find the guy who killed him." Spur slammed out the door and walked a half mile out of town and back. By then he was calmed down enough to think straight. At the sheriff's office he found out who discovered the body and went to talk to him.

The man's name was Nemo Nester, who ran the hardware store. He was up early to get a shipment of bolts and screws and nails put away before opening time. Spur talked to him in the store.

Nester was so farsighted he had glasses to check the invoices against the boxes of goods. He was almost entirely bald, but wore a full beard that was close clipped. His eyes were a soft blue.

"Got up early, Mr. Smith, to come in to the store and I seen this buggy over about two hundred yards from my place. We live out on the edge of town so I can see across the prairie. I like it out there. Nobody bothers us much.

"Anyways, I came out to walk down to the store and I saw the buggy. Wasn't sure whose it was, but right away I saw that the lines weren't tied, and the horse was moving along, grazing and pulling the buggy. That ain't normal. A body's got to figure that something is wrong when that's happening, especially at five in the morning.

"I ran over there, caught the lines which were

trailing and then looked inside. The sheriff lay against the seat, kind of spread out. I could see the powder burns on his shirt. His head was back and his eyes wide open but I could tell right away that he was dead. I took the reins and led the rig down to the sheriff's office and yelled at the deputy.

"But nobody was there. Two of them were out with the posse and the other one must have been home. He come fast when he heard about the killing. That's about it."

"You didn't see anything dropped inside or near the buggy? You didn't take anything out of it?"

"No sir! Wouldn't want to interfere."

"You already did, Mr. Nester. Would you take me out to the exact spot where you saw the rig this morning?"

He called to his clerk to mind the store and they walked out to the area. It was on the west side of town. The last street just ended in the prairie, half a block from the store owner's place. The buggy was another hundred yards into the country from there.

The hardware store man frowned a moment, then walked to where Spur could see buggy tracks turning around in the soft ground.

"Right here. See, that's where I turned the rig around and went back to town."

Spur thanked him and told him he was free to return to his store. Spur spent an hour going over the area. He followed the tracks of the rig back to the street. Saw where the horses had cropped down the grass on its leisurely feed.

He kept looking for footprints. Three or four days ago, there had been a rain in Greensburg and some of the ground was still soft. He checked the whole area from the street out to the turnarond but found no footprints other than those of the horse. Someone could have exited at the end of the hard packed street and left no prints at all.

Spur could find nothing at the end of the street, either. He hoped that something had been dropped or thrown away that could give him a clue. There was nothing at all.

It was the middle of the afternoon, after he had taken a bath in his hotel room in a portable tub, shaved and dressed in clean clothes, that he made the rounds of the saloons, talking with the barkeeps.

It soon became evident that Sheriff Bjelland had taken his usual tour the night he died. That would put him last at the Bar None Saloon.

Mike served Spur a cold tap beer and nodded.

"Yeah, sure, the sheriff was around as usual last night. We talked about his bum leg and the tight bandage the doctor had put on it. They decided it wasn't broke after all, just damn near broke. He was on crutches, but he figured he had to make the circuit."

"He stay long?"

"Oh, about a half hour, as usual. This is . . . was . . . his last stop before he turned in. Things quiet down around here just after midnight. Mostly working folks we have here in town."

"Mike, you remember anybody watching him? Anybody having an argument or a fight with him while he was here?"

"Not a chance. He only talked with me. We had one card game going that didn't end until a little after one. But outside of those four players, wasn't but one or two others in the whole place. I wanted to close up and git."

"The buggy. Any idea whose it was? I forgot to ask the deputy."

"Sure. Belonged to the livery. Some drummer rented it and left it parked in front of the Pride of the Plains Hotel. He left it all ready to go because of an early morning start. He was going to use it today to go out to Hemlock and Roundtree, north of here a ways. No stage goes up there, but there's these two nice little towns where he wanted to show his goods."

"So anybody could have walked along the street, stepped into the rig and driven off."

"Bout the size of it, Mr. Smith."

"Yeah, thanks, Mike." Spur finished his beer slowly, trying to figure it out. He went to the stage office and checked. Five people had left town that morning on the stage heading east. Three more had tickets to go on to Dodge City on the westbound rig that left about an hour ago.

Spur threw down his hat in the sheriff's office. Deputy Sheriff Turner seemed to be in charge. He showed Spur the map of the state. The next town of any size was Dodge City.

"A problem?" Turner asked.

"Somewhat. Let's say you are the killer I'm hunting. You've just killed the lawmen in the five towns behind us toward Wichita. What town would you pick for your next victim, moving on west?"

"No doubt. Dodge City. Nothing worthwhile between here and there. Not even a full time lawman. Some parttimers. One little place has a barber who is also town marshal. Another one has the mayor, who doubles as the town marshal and he's also the operator of the livery stable."

"My man is probably already on his way to Dodge City. I'll be out of here tomorrow. You turn up anything you wire me care of the sheriff in Dodge City."

Spur ate a large early dinner and showed up at the Bar None Saloon for some serious poker playing. He had fifty dollars that he hoped he might lose. Then he would feel a lot better about getting out of town tomorrow just after noon on the westbound stage.

He played poker and drank beer. Damn! He hated to be beaten by the killer. He killed Bjelland right under Spur's nose! It could even be someone he had seen in town. More likely the man held in the background, watched the routine of the sheriff and planned his strike. The bank robbery and two deputies gunning out of town had been made to order for him. Damn!

"Hey, mister, I just raised a dollar," a voice jabbed at him from across the poker table. "You in this pot or not?"

McCoy threw in a chip and stared at his cards. He won the pot and was twelve dollars ahead.

They stopped the game and Lila came on to sing. She had put in several new songs tonight and finished with a song Spur had never heard before, "Empty Arms And A Crying Heart."

By the time Lila came on to sing at the eleven o'clock show, Spur was ten dollars losers. He folded, kept his chair for the show and then waited for Lila.

She had seen him in his chair down front. He played solitaire as he waited.

"Red queen will play on your king of spades," a familiar voice said to him over his shoulder. He turned and stood.

"Lila, you were great tonight, as usual."

"Thank you. Going back to the hotel?" She seemed rather subdued as he nodded.

"Lost all my money, time to leave."

"You still have your horse, saddle and rifle."

"Not even that, rifle is all, I guess."

Outside she caught his arm and pulled close to him.

"This time of night still makes me shiver," she said. "I guess it goes back to my childhood. I always was afraid of the dark."

Then went up the stairs and straight to her room. She gave him the key, he opened the door and she waved him inside. As soon as Spur lit the lamp, she closed the door and locked it, then she put her arms around his neck and pulled his face down so she could kiss him.

The kiss was serious. Her lips parted and her tongue darted at his lips, then inside his mouth. She sighed and pressed against him. She broke it off and led him to the bed where she sat down.

"The other night, did you think I was drunk?"

"You did have several glasses of wine."

"I knew exactly what I was doing, even when I took off my dress. I never let it change the way I treated you. I'm sorry I was so tired. I really just went to sleep." She reached over and unbuttoned the soft leather vest he wore over his shirt.

"Right now I know exactly what I'm doing, too. I want you to stay in my bed tonight. I want us to make love together. Yes, together. Making love is a cooperating thing. Nobody assaults the other one. Together we explore and caress and then at last we come together to our mutual satisfaction."

She kissed him again where he sat beside her. Gently she pressed him back on the bed and leaned over on top of him.

"First we do a lot of kissing and petting, and then if we both are pleased, we will undress each other."

She leaned up to watch him carefully. "Is that way of making love all right with you?"

"Absolutely. It's a beautiful system, it's poetry."

"Maybe you won't like me naked."

"You were half-naked the other night, and I loved what I saw."

Lila giggled. "You didn't even start to love any of me, but before tonight's over we're going to love each other to pieces!"

She bent and kissed him again, lying fully on top of him, pressing her breasts against his chest. She caught one of his hands and put it between them covering a breast.

"They do love to be petted." She kissed him again, devouring his open mouth. "Oh, did I tell you? Tonight was my last night. I'm going to Dodge City tomorrow. It was all arranged weeks ago. A booking agent in St. Louis set it up for me by mail."

Spur's hand rubbed her breast through the fabric of her dress. He felt her nipple swell and the heat came through the cloth.

"I'm heading for Dodge City tomorrow, myself.

Perhaps we can sit together on the stage?"

"I'll count on it." She kissed him again. "But that won't be near the marvelous, wonderful experience that we're having now, and that we're going to have until morning!" She sat up and began to open the buttons down his shirt front. Her hand slipped inside and played with the black hair on his chest.

"I love a man with hair on his chest," she said then pressed back his shirt and kissed his chest, biting tenderly on his man nipples.

He sat up and opened the top buttons of her soft blue dress.

"Did I tell you that you're the prettiest lady I've seen in a dozen months of Sundays?" She shook her head. "You are, you have a marvelous smile, dancing eyes, a little nose that turns up just a smidgen, and a mouth that is delightful when open or closed."

She helped him slip the dress off her shoulders. He sucked in a quick breath. The chemise she wore over her binder was of soft blue lace, so delicate it looked as if it might blow away, yet sturdy and protective. He touched it and she smiled.

"You liked the white lace chemise the other night, too. It was interesting to watch you as I took off my dress. I wondered what you would do. I made a little bet with myself that you wouldn't 'take advantage of me' in my evidently tipsy situation."

"You won." He leaned in and breathed his hot breath through the lace and into the binder that covered her breasts.

"Oh, lordy but that is nice!" she said softly. Quickly she lifted up on her knees on the bed and

77

pulled the dress over her head. His hands covered both her breasts and she slid toward him.

"You have no idea how wonderful that makes me feel."

He lifted the chemise and pushed his hand under it, sliding under the wrapper until his fingers closed around her bare left breast and he squeezed her pulsating nipple.

"Oh, glory! Colt, I want you to kiss me just ever so long!"

He did and she moved her hand down his bare chest to his crotch, found the swelling there and rubbed it through the trousers.

After several minutes she lifted up from him, pulled the chemise over her head and then quickly took off the wrapper letting her breasts swing free.

Spur sat there staring. "So beautiful! The wonder of a woman's breasts always amazes me. So perfectly sculptured, so wonderful!"

His hand moved toward one and she breathed deeply in anticipation. He barely touched her skin below her breasts, rubbed gently, then moved upward to the swell and tenderly traced a line around her mound.

Lila sighed and leaned toward him more, so her breasts hung nearly straight down. They were large, with heavy soft pink areolas and throbbing dark red nipples.

He caressed the breast, working slowly around it until he came to her nipple. Her eyes were closed. Spur bent and kissed the small bit of extended flesh, then licked it and at last pulled as much of her breast into his mouth as he could.

Her hips bucked convulsively and she jolted into a climax that rattled her and kept her hips pounding upward toward him for almost a minute. Her breath came in ragged gasps and the tremors slowed and then faded away.

Slowly her eyes opened and she pushed her arms around him and clung to him, her breasts against his bare chest.

"Oh, God, never . . . never in my life have I ever exploded that way before . . . before you were inside me. Marvelous!"

He kissed her other breast, then pulled at her petticoats. She took them off and then her stocking and shoes and sat there, proud in her bare top and white drawers that had small pink bows on them.

Spur stepped to the door, made sure it was locked and came back. He walked to the bed and she hugged his waist, then kissed the bulge in his pants.

"Show me," she said. She sat on the bed shivering, not knowing what to do with her hands. "I'm so nervous I can hardly wait," she said softly.

Spur opened the fly buttons and turned, pulled down his pants and short underwear and kicked them off. Then he turned.

His erection was full, ready. It stabbed out from him at a angle. Lila gave a small cry of delight and grabbed his shaft. She was so gentle he hardly knew she held him. Slowly and with her eyes wide, she lowered her head toward him and kissed the thick, purple head.

Lila shivered. "Sweet damn! sweet damn! sweet damn! I've never seen one so wonderful, and so big. Lordy, he'll never fit inside my little cunny." Lila giggled. "Lordy, lordy!"

She sat on the side of the bed and quickly unbuttoned her drawers and began to pull them down. He stopped her. Gently he pressed her back on the bed and moved his hands to the white material that was still at her waist.

He pulled down the material. Soon the gentle swell of her flat belly showed and after another inch he revealed the top of her pubic hair. Spur kissed the spot, moving the cloth down a little at a time, kissing it down her legs until her entire "V" of soft brown hair showed.

He pushed his face into the muff, found her moist spot and kissed it.

"Oh, God!" she screeched. She put her hand over her mouth, surprise on her face, a look of absolute worship wreathing her features.

"Lordy, nobody ever did that for me before!"

He took her drawers off and then lay beside her on the bed. At first they didn't touch, then her hand stretched out.

"Please, Colt Smith. Please love me!"

Spur touched her breasts, caressed them, leaned down and kissed them both, then turned her gently to her back. She shook her head.

"No, the other way." She lifted over him and lay on his stomach, kissing him all over his face, then at last on his open mouth.

Slowly he lifted her hips, moved her down, then adjusted his shaft and lowered her to meet him.

"Oh . . . oh . . . Colt . . . that's good . . . so . . . so . . ."

For a moment he thought she had passed out.

Then her face blossomed over his with a wonderful smile. "So wonderful!" She had been holding herself up. Now she lowered and Spur felt his lance penetrating deeply into her.

Lila moaned in joy, lifted and dropped suddenly impaling herself to the very last tenth of an inch.

"Oh, lord if I'm going to die soon anyway, let it be right now!"

Spur chuckled. "I've never heard it put that way before," he said.

She didn't bother to answer. She lifted up and came down. Her face showed the kind of pleasure that was beyond all measure. She repeated the movement and soon set up a rhythm that kept her rocking and riding over him like a jockey on a thundering race horse.

Perspiration beaded on her forehead and a salty drop hit Spur on the lip. He grinned, moved his hands so he could play with her bouncing, rocking big breasts. He felt a stirring deep within himself but knew he could control it, make it last for a long time.

After a dozen more strokes he wasn't so sure that he could last. Lila closed her eyes and growled, then the throbbing, thundering climax hit her and her whole body rattled like a rabbit in a dog's mouth. She shook and trembled as one series after another of spasms pulsated through her, making her hips dance and pound down on him a dozen times without any control.

She wailed softly, dropped her chest to his and kissed him furiously for the last half of the long climax.

Just as she was about to taper off, Spur's own floodgates opened and the river of molten lava flowed through the valve and jetted from his shaft like a liquid metal geyser, splashing into her, setting her off on another series of climaxes, even as he trembled and his whole body stiffened as he drove upward as high as he could, lifting her and himself off the bed, bowing up until the very last drop of seed shot from him and he collapsed on the bed, panting, trying to get in enough air to live on as the mini death claimed him.

She lifted up to look at him a moment. Lila snuggled on top of him, secure in her womanhood, glad that she could satisfy him, delighted that he was so gentle, so tender, that he had made love with her, not simply taken her.

She moved her hips gently, feeling him inside her, then to her sorrow she felt him shrinking. She gripped him with her muscles, trying to excite him again.

Spur laughed gently. "Don't worry, sexy little lady, there is lots more. We are only beginning a long, exciting night. I do need a ten minute recuperation time. Do you still have that bottle of wine?"

She was up and away from him in a second. She bounced all bare and delightful to the dresser and came back with two bottles.

Spur smiled. It was going to be a great night that would make up for a terrible day. Tomorrow. He would worry about catching a killer in Dodge City tomorrow.

7

Spur McCoy woke up in Lila's bed the next morning. It was just after daylight. She snuggled against his side, one arm across his chest. He caught one of her breasts and rubbed it gently. She stirred, smiled, but continued sleeping. He bent and kissed her bare breast and she came awake slowly.

"Once more!" Lila said with a savage snarl. "Once more quick—fast and mean!"

He rolled over her and thrust and she cried out. Then they began pounding against each other as though it was the first time and they both climaxed quickly, then lay together panting and laughing and grinning and talking.

"It's never been so good for me," Lila said. "Sure I like sex, I like to get fucked, but this has been something tremendously special for me. I know you'll be moving on, but I'll never forget you, Colt Smith."

He held her close. "How could I ever forget a lady who sings like a nightingale and makes love like a tiger!"

They had another nap, got up and dressed and went down to breakfast. After that Spur checked in at the sheriff's office but there wasn't much he could do. Absolutely no clues about who killed Sheriff Bjelland. Before he left, a rider came in. He was from south a ways, he said, from Coldwater.

The rider was lean, sunburned, all cowhand.

"Heading out to Montana where my uncle lives," the man said. "Yeah, pardon me. My name is Eugene Gregg and I work cattle. Rode up to sell my horse and catch the stage west and north. Don't know the best way."

He turned the well worn hat in his hands. "What I really want to tell you is that the sheriff down at Coldwater got himself killed couple of days ago. Don't know how it happened, but thought I should tell you, you being another sheriff and all that."

"How was he killed?" Spur asked, at once alert.

"Don't rightly know. Shot, I know that for sure. I was on the Bar Y spread and didn't hear about it until I got to town. Only about twenty miles down there. Guess that's another county, but I'm not too sure."

"But the sheriff was shot dead?"

"Right about that, I saw his body." The cowboy hesitated. "Well, I guess I better get to the stage and buy myself a ticket. Oh, where is the livery?"

The deputy pointed the way and the cowboy thanked them and headed for the livery barn to sell his horse. Spur rubbed his jaw. "There was time. Our man could have lit out on a horse the night he killed Sheriff Bjelland, had lots of time to get there and bushwhacked the sheriff down in Coldwater the next day. I've got to go down and check on it."

Spur looked at Deputy Turner. "Good luck here, and if you hear anything, send word to the sheriff in Dodge City."

They shook hands and Spur hurried out the door, his jaw set in a determined pose that was half anger, half frustration.

He found Lila in her room and only half dressed.

"Once more?" she said with a grin. Spur shook his head.

"Sorry, I won't be able to ride to Dodge City with you. I have to grab a horse and ride south." He told her about the problem and that he wanted to find out what happened.

"For being a land buyer, you seem terribly concerned about these lawmen."

"Curious, mostly. The stability of a town affects the price of land. A place like Dodge City with its strong lawmen, is much better for land speculation than say, Tombstone, Arizona, where there is hardly any law at all."

Spur wasn't sure he had convinced her. "I'll see you in our room in Dodge City." He kissed her, lingering over the task. "No sense in renting two rooms when we use just one."

She smiled, nodded and waved as he hurried out the door.

Spur packed his gear, went to the livery and rented a horse. He left his carpetbag at the hotel but took his rifle along. It was only twenty two miles to Coldwater. A little over four hours at a good canter. He'd try it.

The bay he rode was strong and steady and loved

to canter along at her natural gait eating up the miles. He stopped at what he figured was halfway and ate the two sandwiches he had had them make for him in the hotel kitchen. There was no time to boil coffee.

He arrived in the small community of Coldwater just after two o'clock. There couldn't be more than two hundred people in the town. It was ranching country.

He rode directly to the small courthouse and the sheriff's office. It was locked.

The county clerk came down the short hall.

"Yep, thought I heard somebody come in. Might be I can help a bit, I'm the county clerk."

"The sheriff. I heard he was shot."

"True, the Caruther Boys. Got a little rowdy and skunk drunk in the Silver Spur Saloon three nights ago and shot up the place. Sheriff Downing went in to calm things down and they shot him dead before he could say howdy."

"Did they escape?"

"Yep, for a day and a half. Then our posse tracked them down and did some shooting of themselves. Killed Jed and shot up Willy bad. If he lives, he'll be hanged in three days. Had the trial yesterday."

"No wasted time. I like that."

"Anything else? I'm the county staff today. The other two are off inspecting or something. Danged place is getting top heavy with workers."

Spur thought of the thousands and thousands of government employees in Washington, D.C., and he smiled. "Yes, sir, I guess it can do that. Thanks for the information."

Spur walked down the main street, which was called Gulch Lane, until he found a small restaurant. He knew he should start back. He might be able to catch the stage. One look at his pocket watch told him the stage was just leaving. He'd be on the one tomorrow.

He had two cups of coffee and treated himself to two pieces of homemade cherry pie. It was the best he'd had in months. Spur took a half mile walk, came back to his horse. He looked over his rig a minute, then stopped at the hardware store for a quart sized canteen with a carrying case. He filled the canteen from the public pump at the far end of town, and hit the trail. With any luck he should be into Greensburg just before dark.

It had been a wild goose chase coming down here. But he knew it might be that when he left. In his position he had to double check every possibility, run down every chance. That's why the killer always had the advantage. Spur felt he was getting closer. Maybe he could nail the bastard before he killed again.

When Spur arrived back in Greensburg that evening, he returned the horse, rented a room and enjoyed a long hot bath. Then he talked to Deputy Turner, found out there were no clues of any kind to the sheriff's death and turned in for an early bedtime. He had to recoup his strength from last night. Now that was a delightful kind of a problem to have.

McCoy smiled as he thought of the enthusiastic, inventive and insatiable way that Lila enjoyed making love. He looked forward to more of her love-making when he got to Dodge City and found the little songbird again.

The long stage ride did nothing for his bad mood when he stepped off the rig in Dodge City slightly after dark the next evening. He had thought of absolutely no new means to smoke out the killer. Spur had rejected the idea of setting up the sheriff as bait for the killer and then catching him just before he pulled the trigger. It was too risky.

He tried at two hotels before he found the one where Lila had registered. He took a room for two nights, paid the outrageous sum of two dollars for the two nights and went up to the second floor.

Lila was on the third, her favorite. She said she liked to look out over the lights of a town and discover how far into the plains she could see.

He put his gear in his room, washed up and shaved closely, then knocked on Lila's door. She wasn't in. It was just past 6:30. Maybe she was having a late supper downstairs in the hotel dining room.

Spur stood at the entrance to the dining room and looked over the supper crowd. The room was about half filled. He spotted Lila at a table for two in the far corner. Spur made a roundabout trip so she wouldn't see him come up.

He stood behind her chair.

"Miss, it's terribly crowded tonight, would you mind sharing your table with a hungry person?"

Lila looked up, beaming at him, her smile so genuine and fresh that he bent and kissed her cheek, then sat down. She reached for his hand.

"I missed you. What took you so long?"

"Slowing down in my old age. Do you sing tonight?"

She nodded. "At eight and ten at the Silver Dollar Gambling Emporium. I told him I would sing twice a night. He finally agreed. He had a letter from Mike telling him about his increase in business.

"I also raised my rate to twenty-five dollars a week! I'm making as much in a week as most cowboys make in a month!"

"You must have earned a lot more in the big music halls in the East."

"Yes, but that became boring after a while. I didn't want to join one of those traveling shows with singing and dancing. I don't dance at all, and I'm not an actress. So I decided to come out into the Wild West and see for myself what it's all about. You know, it isn't as scary as I thought it would be. Of course I haven't even seen an Indian or a buffalo."

"You're afraid of buffalos?"

"No, silly, but I want to see some, just so I can say I saw them out here."

"And are you learning lots out here in the big bad, Wild, Wild West?"

"Mostly from a man who was raised in New York City!"

She hadn't ordered. Here the menu was much broader than it had been in Greensburg and they took some time to figure out what they wanted.

After the meal Spur escorted her up to her room where she said she needed to lie down for a while before she sang. She always did.

Spur went down the street to the sheriff's office.
He had been here before and knew the sheriff, Frank
Johnson, a tough, smart lawman who had been in
dozens of shooting scrapes and always came out of
them.

"McCoy! Thought you might be around
somewhere. Heard about Bjelland. Didn't know
him, but I hate to see any lawman go down. Five in a
row back toward Wichita?"

Johnson was a tall man with a paunch that turned
into a beer belly, but his belt still held up his pants.
He seldom wore a gun now, dealing out his toughest
assignments to quick, young men who wore deputy
badges.

They went into Johnson's small office.

"Frank, on this trip I'm Colt Smith. Be obliged if
you could call me that. Trying to stay low key as a
land buyer. You know of any good deals in land I can
look at around here to help make me look
legitimate?"

"But you're really working on this lawman killer,
right? I can call you Colt for a spell. The important
thing is that I'm probably next in line for that damn
killer. From everything I can hear and from what
the broadsides say, this killer is the sneaky kind.
Not a stand up and shoot it out, but a sly, slick
sneaker who always shoots his victims in the gut
first from point blank range."

"That's about it. Try always to have a deputy
with you wherever you go, even to the outhouse. The
better your protection, the longer you're going to
live. I hope we can get this guy caught in a day or
two. I keep looking for some gunman I've seen in the

towns before this one, but I can't spot anybody so far."

"Keep looking." The sheriff laughed nervously. "Keep a deputy with me all the time. You mean my deputy has to go to bed with me and Milly, too?"

Spur grinned. "Damn right, but he can sleep on your side and Milly on the other side." Spur paused. "Unless, of course, Milly wants to be in the middle!"

They both laughed, but each knew the importance of their talk. Spur left a few minutes later.

Just outside the sheriff's office he jolted to a stop. Across the street was a drummer he remembered seeing in two of the previous towns. Yes, the drummer would have a legitimate reason for being here, he had clients and customers to sell his line to, whatever it might be.

But that would also be a good cover-up for a murderous trail. Spur went across the street behind the man, and followed him. He did not have his sample case. He had even untied his string tie, but still had on his white shirt and his black businessman's suit.

The drummer was average height, a little bit on the well fed side and the brown hair on top of his head had thinned to the point of providing a palm-sized bald spot.

The drummer turned in at a saloon and Spur followed him. He had a beer, then sat in on a game of poker. It wasn't his game. He lost every hand and even though it was a dime limit, he quickly lost three dollars and shook his head. He pushed back from the table and bowed out.

The salesman went down the boardwalk, stared in

windows and stopped in the next saloon, a larger one with gambling and six fancy ladies who danced and served drinks and flipped on their backs in the cribs upstairs for "one dollar straight, and two dollars all fancy and wild."

Spur's target had two shots of whiskey, then grabbed the first girl who walked past and headed for the closed stairway that led to the cribs.

Spur waited. Actually he timed the drummer. He was gone exactly twenty-two minutes. He came down with a smile on his face, had another beer and settled in at a nickel limit poker game.

The salesman's luck had changed and before long he was winning. By midnight he had outlasted all the other players and asked for a cloth bag to put all the dimes, nickels, quarters and one and two dollar gold pieces in. No paper money was allowed on that table.

There were few people on the Dodge streets after midnight. Spur saw two patrolling sheriff deputies who tried store doors, urged drunks on their way home, and generally surveyed their domain.

The drummer ignored them. He had downed about four beers during the evening, but was not drunk. He walked steadily and went past the sheriff's office, stopped and looked in through the barred doors, then continued to a smaller hotel and went up the steps and vanished inside.

Spur saw a light come on in one of the second floor windows, then the drummer looked out the window for a moment and closed the curtains.

Good night, sweet prince.

Spur gave it up. If the man were going to do anything suspicious, it would have been after midnight. But he didn't even try to see the sheriff. The head lawman had agreed to stay in the jail for the next few nights, just to be on the safe side. No sense taking any chance. His wife's sister was staying with her and the kids.

The drummer had not made a false move. What else was there for a visiting salesman but beer, whiskey, a naked fancy lady and a little poker?

Spur went back to his room and tensed when he saw light coming from under his door. He touched the doorknob and turned it slowly, silently. It was not locked. He drew his long barreled .45 and thrust the door open in one quick move, his .45 covering the room.

The only person in the room was Lila Pemberthy. She sat on the bed wearing what looked like a pale yellow shift made entirely of expensive lace. She pouted like a spoiled little girl when she saw him.

"I hate you, Colt Smith!" Lila said. "You didn't even come and hear me sing tonight! I should never even talk to you again, let alone undress for you."

"Sorry, I was busy. I had to see several men on business. I'll listen tomorrow night."

"Then you don't hate me?"

"Of course not. Just the opposite." He closed the door, locked it and pushed the .45 back in leather.

"For really and truly?"

"Absolutely."

She lifted up on her knees on the bed. The yellow lace traced a shifting pattern over her surging breasts. As she lifted on her knees, the shift rose over her waist and revealed the soft brown "V" of hair.

"Then come and show me that you love me, right now!" She held out her arms.

Spur smiled and unbuckled his gunbelt and dropped it on the dresser as he walked toward her. He put his arms around her and bent her slowly backward on the bed, resting on top of her slender, sexy body.

"I know just how to prove to you that I don't hate you," McCoy said softly.

Lila kissed his nose and then his eyes and lastly his soft lips.

"You're going to have to prove that at least three times tonight," she said. Then she began kissing him again.

8

The next morning's stage brought in some mail from Kansas City for Spur McCoy, in care of the sheriff's office. Spur checked in with the law people just after breakfast. A big envelope contained eight wanted posters. Each one had a note on it fastened with a straight pin.

All eight of the men pictured had been arrested at one time or another by one or more of the five lawmen murdered in Kansas within the last six weeks.

Spur laid them out on the sheriff's desk and they went over the names. Spur had heard of all of them, had chased and not caught two.

Slowly Spur began to shake his head. "It just doesn't work, Frank. These men are wanted, some of them killers, and granted they might have hated some of the dead lawmen. But the fact remains that one man killed all six of the men. It's exactly the same method, the same kind of gun, the same placement of the shots, and the whole set of circumstances are almost identical."

Frank Johnson leaned back in his chair and scratched his thinning hair.

"Hadn't heard that, about the same method."

"Powder burns on every shot made. My guess is the first round is in the gut to put the man down and helpless. Then when the murderer is ready to finish the job, he puts the muzzle over the victim's heart and pulls the trigger again."

McCoy stared at the pictures. "All but one of these outlaws are stand up shooters. They'll go toe to toe with you with their six-guns, but they'd rather be away from you ten or fifteen feet."

"These flyers don't help a rat's ass, then, do they?" Sheriff Johnson asked.

"Afraid not."

The sheriff bunched the wanted posters and put them in a drawer with a hundred others.

"You know anything about one of the drummers in town, Sheriff? This one is average height, bald on top. I don't know what he's selling."

"We get half a dozen a week through here. They must sell something. Most of them give us no trouble at all. The trail crews are the ones we watch out for."

"I'll do some more checking. He's the one man I've seen in more than one of these towns where the lawman was killed. Oh, I'd say you're free as a bird during the day. It's nighttime when this killer strikes. After dark, I don't want you to wiggle out of the jail without at least one deputy guarding you."

Spur left the sheriff's office and checked the register at the Dodge House Hotel where he had seen the salesman go in last night. The desk clerk said they only had one salesman, a Mr. Jonas Kelly from St. Louis, who sold fine kitchen cutlery and sporting knives.

"How can I find him?"

"Beats me. Wait, he did say something about selling to his wholesale customers first. He just got in yesterday, so I'd guess he's at the stores. Hardware maybe."

Spur thanked the clerk and walked two blocks to the Dodge Hardware. It was a good sized establishment, with almost everything a farmer or rancher needed except food. But the drummer wasn't there. A clerk said he might be next door at the saddlery.

He was. Spur spotted him at once, went in and looked at a hand tooled saddle. It was a beauty. The saddlemaker was inlaying additional silver in it. It wasn't new. By now the silver in it alone must be worth a lot of money.

"I said I'll take two of those small knives," the saddlemaker said. "That's all I need. You know I don't sell retail."

"I can give you a real good price."

"Enough! You were here six months ago and loaded me up with more knives than I can use. If you don't want to sell me those two, forget it."

Spur wandered out. The drummer was a real salesman, and he had been here six months ago. Not a chance he could be the chain-linked murderer.

For an hour Spur wandered the town. Dodge was growing. Lots of new stores and houses had been built since he was there last. Many more people. Which made more problems for him. More people meant more individuals to watch, more places for the real killer to hide.

He stood in front of the hotel for half an hour, watching the citizens pass by. One man he followed for two blocks. The man seemed familiar, as if he had seen the same face before. He wore a suit, with proper vest, gold chain and watch fob. He also could be hiding a derringer.

Then the man took out a key and opened the door to a dry goods store. He was probably the owner—not the killer Spur searched for.

Spur bought a deck of playing cards at the Dodge Mercantile and went back to the hotel. He went directly to Lila's room and knocked. She opened the door a crack to see who it was, then swung it wide.

She held a pink dress in front of her as Spur closed the door.

"Colt, marvelous lover. Do you like me in this pink?" She tossed the dress aside and she wore nothing at all. She grinned and grabbed a blue dress and held it in front of her. "Or do I look better in the blue?"

"The blue," Spur said surprised at the sudden show of naked flesh. He went over to the window and looked out, then back at Lila who had let the dress fall and stood there deliciously topless, smiling at him.

"It was a special surprise for you," she said. "I was watching out the window and I saw you coming up the street with that determined, no nonsense stride. I knew you were coming here."

She cupped both her breasts and held them up toward him.

"Hungry?"

He went to her and took her in his arms and hugged her properly, then released her.

"Lila, you're beautiful, you're a marvelous lover, and I like to be with you. But right now we need to talk, and I can talk to you lots easier if your beautiful, sexy charms are covered with a dress."

Lila giggled and put on the blue dress, but buttoned up only a few of the front fasteners so her breasts peeked out as she moved.

He took out the cards and sat cross-legged on the bed.

"We're going to play gin rummy and talk. I want to know all about you, and I'll even tell you more about me. I need to get some things settled in my mind, and I like to play gin rummy as I'm thinking. Would that be all right?"

"Of course. But you have to kiss me first."

He did. She won five straight hands of gin rummy. Spur couldn't keep his mind on the game. It wandered to new and wild ways to catch the killer, but none of them seemed practical. Maybe he should ask the sheriff to pretend to be bait for the killer's trap. Set up some kind of lonely vigil.

No!

He could have the sheriff locked up in a jail cell every night! Yes, that would help. There were enough officers here so there was always one man at the jail during the evening hours. Another walked on patrol out in the streets. They changed places at midnight or some such hour. That might work.

Spur held the cards. "Now, the other day you told me you were born in Louisiana. How did you get started singing? Did you take lessons?''

"All right, I'll tell you," Lila said. "Nobody has ever been interested before. I sang in the church choir when I was in school, and one day I saw a traveling troupe of singers and dancers and I told my mother that's what I wanted to do. She ignored me. When I was sixteen, I ran away from home and worked in a small store in New Orleans and learned how to sing.

"I was married for a short time, and then I went back to singing, and got better and went to St. Louis and Chicago, and I've made a modest success. That's about all of it."

"How old were you when you were married?"

"Seventeen, but my husband was killed in an accident and since then I've concentrated on singing."

"You're good," Spur said. "You could sing in New York and Washington if you wanted to. I could give you a letter. . . .''

She shook her head. "No, I'm here now and I'll stay for a while. I've waited a long time to look at the West, so now I want to see all of it."

She jumped off the bed and let one breast pop through the half closed dress. Lila watched him, grinning.

Spur laughed. "You just never get enough, do you? I'd love to but you used me up this morning. Besides, it's noon and time to have a bite somewhere. Let's find a little restaurant out of the hotel."

She finished dressing and they went out to eat. It was a small cafe beside the Dodge Mercantile, with only six tables and the food had a decided German accent. They had big sausages smothered in sauerkraut, toast and jelly and coffee.

"That's the strangest meal I've ever eaten," Lila said. She told him it was time for her afternoon rest before she sang, and he walked her back to her room. She pulled him inside, kissed him deliciously and let him rub her breasts. Then she smiled.

"Now I think I can have a nap without dreaming that you are making love to me."

Spur went to the sheriff's office, but there was no report of any contact by a weird person with the sheriff. McCoy watched Frank Johnson for a minute, then plunged ahead.

"I have an idea. What would you think of having yourself locked up every night at ten in the evening, with strict instructions you don't get out of the cell unless the jailhouse is burning down."

"I hate the idea. I don't like to be locked up." Frank scowled and lit is pipe. "But I think it's a damn fine idea. If I can't get out in the dark, nobody is going to bushwhack me." The sheriff frowned. "We'll try it for five or six days, no more. If your killer hasn't made his play by then, I'm going to decide that he's done with his chain link killings of lawmen."

"Sounds fair to me, Sheriff. I had thought of displaying you in a black buggy as bait . . . ." He watched the lawman.

"That's what we'll do if this week of incarceration don't work. At least I can get my work done during the day."

Loud voices in the outer office brought both men

out of their chairs and through the door.

Two men stood arguing with a deputy. He turned and lifted a hand in resignation and turned to the sheriff.

"The matter of water rights again, I'm afraid, Sheriff. Scotty MacDougal is at it again."

"Sheriff, you told us the next time it happened you'd arrest that son-of-a-bitch," the taller of the two men said. They both looked like ranchers which they were. "Now is the time, Frank. He damned up Amber Creek again."

Sheriff Johnson stood there a minute. Then he brightened. "Yeah, I got a solution. Men, I'd like you to meet Colt Smith. Special deputy of mine. Colt, this is Dick Hendricks, and Horace Eagleton, ranchers out of town, a ways to the north.

"Gentlemen, I can't get out there right now, but I can send Smith here. He'll take care of the matter, work it out somehow. If he has to arrest Scotty, then so be it. I want this thing settled once and for all."

Spur pulled Sheriff Johnson back down the short hall.

"What the hell? I can't go chasing around the countryside. I got a killer to nail."

"If you don't go, I got to go. Take your pick. Me safe in jail here or out there in the dark where I might get bushwhacked and it would be all your fault."

Spur growled. He was boxed in with nowhere to retreat. "Three ranches on one stream and the top man is damming up the water?"

"Yep."

"Kansas have an irrigation rights law?"

"Yep, and Scotty knows all about it."

"Damn! This could take two or three days . . ."

"You should be back in time for supper. Only about six miles out to the top spread."

"Hell! Loan me a horse and a rifle. Might as well get it over with and get back to my main job."

9

Spur McCoy and the two ranchers were halfway to
the Scotty MacDougal Ranch before the men
calmed down. They were mad and they wanted some
action. In two or thee days they would start to lose
some of their cattle.

McCoy had stopped by at the hardware on their
way and picked up six sticks of dynamite,
detonators and fuses. That was in case there was a
damn across the creek that needed blasting. They
would take shovels from the Hendricks Ranch since
it was closest to the suspected dam.

"He always does this," Horace Eagleton said.
"Just because he was here first he thinks he owns
God."

"About the size of it," Hendricks said. "This time
we put him in his place for good, or he gets
arrested!"

At the Hendricks place they stopped for a cold
drink of water, took shovels and moved up through
the trees along the stream so nobody from the Mac-
Dougal spread could see them.

Amber Creek here was just about that, maybe a foot deep and fifteen feet across. But now it was nearly dry, an occasional low spot still held pools of water. Normally it would have a good current and a lot of water would go down it.

"I get so mad I could spit every time I see the creek this way!" Hendricks snorted. "Damn his eyes!"

"This time we've got the old bastard," Eagleton said, grinning.

Spur wanted only to get this over with and ride back to Dodge City to catch his killer. But sometimes things got a little out of order. He wasn't quite sure what to do yet. When he saw exactly how the water was diverted, he could decide.

They rode another half hour, passed within a quarter mile of a spread the men said was Mac-Dougal's. Then they came out at a natural little lake.

"So that's how he done it," Hendricks said. "Used to be an old lake here a hundred years ago. Good grazing. MacDougal must have cut a new channel, diverting the water from Amber Creek into the old lake bed. Damn thing is huge. He can take all of our water for the rest of the summer."

They rode faster then, along the side of Amber Creek and next to the filling lake.

"There it is!" Hendricks said.

They pulled to a stop at the top of the lake where it was at almost the same level as the stream. A two-foot-wide ditch had been dug through the bank for a distance of not over ten or twelve feet. From there the water found a natural course into the dry lake bed.

Spur eyed it for a minute.

"Glad we brought the spades," Spur said. "Let's fill in the ditch."

The three men dismounted and began throwing the dirt and rocks back into the ditch that had been dug out. The water washed most of them away in the current.

Spur stopped. "We need some brush or old logs to jam in there first," he said.

They found the brush easily, hacked off some more with belt knives, and then Spur discovered an old rotting log that he kicked to pieces and carried the two foot long sections to the ditch.

Now, with a foundation to hold the dirt, it was a much easier job to throw dirt in front of the logs and brush to start making a dam across the ditch.

After an hour of hard work, all but a trickle of water from Amber Creek was flowing downstream in its natural bed again. The men wiped brows.

"We better find a defensive position," Spur said. "My guess is that as soon as MacDougal sees the water coming down the creek again, he'll come storming up here with some help."

All three men had rifles with them. They went to the far side of the stream about fifty yards above, hid their horses in the brush out of the line of fire, and settled down to wait. Spur found a cottonwood tree that gave him fine protection. The other two used old logs and a small rise of ground for their fortifications.

"How long it going to take?" Spur asked.

"Old Scotty stays pretty close around his ranch

buildings lately," Eagleton said. "He'll spot the water coming down quick, I'd guess."

An hour later nothing had happened. Spur pulled his pocket watch and read the time. Almost three o'clock. At three-thirty Spur slapped his thigh.

"Hell, we better go down there and talk to Scotty," Spur said.

"Not a chance," Hendricks spat. "He'll shoot us as soon as he sees us."

"Not me," Spur said. "He doesn't know who I am. You two can stay in the brush."

"Worth a try," Eagleton said with a twinkle in his eye. "If he kills you we'll ride back and tell the sheriff."

Before they headed for their horses, Spur caught movement on a slope across the stream.

"Company," Spur said. The rider left the open rise and angled into the fringe of brush along the stream. Three minutes later he walked his roan up to edge of the filled in diversion ditch.

"That's Scotty," Hendricks said.

Spur stood up quickly.

"Mr. MacDougal. I'm with the sheriff's office and notifying you that the ditch you dug there is against the law, so I filled it in. You do not have irrigation rights to all the water from this creek. One third is yours, the rest goes downstream."

Spur didn't see the man draw his six-gun, but it thundered in the early afternoon. At once one of the men beside him fired a rifle and Scotty MacDougal screamed and rolled out of sight.

Spur stepped behind his tree.

"Who fired that shot? All he has is a pistol and

we're out of range."

"Seen a man killed once at a hundred yards with a six-gun slug," Hendricks said. "Taking no chances."

Spur called again. "Scotty, we have to talk. Are you hit bad?"

Four rounds answered Spur, the lead flying harmlessly into the ground well in front of them.

"Scotty, my name is Colt Smith. Sheriff Johnson sent me out here as an impartial observer to straighten this out. There'll be no charges against you if you throw out your six-gun and sit on the bank so I can come up there and talk."

"All right! Damn bushwhackers. Who was it shot me?"

"Throw out your gun, Scotty."

Spur saw a weapon come over the bank. He left his tree and with the rifle under his arm, walked slowly up to the small diversion ditch they had filled in.

Scotty MacDougal lay on the far side. He had just tied up the wound in his leg and glared at Spur.

"Got to be Hendricks and Eagleton, right? Them bastards!"

"MacDougal, you know I could arrest you right now and take you into jail for diverting this water. You know it's illegal, so why did you do it?"

"Damn fancy new laws. In my time a man owned the water on his spread."

"Still do if it's a lake with no outlet. A running stream is not property, MacDougal. It comes under the fair use irrigation law, which you know about."

MacDougal glared at Spur. "Tell me, Hendricks and Eagleton over there with you, right?"

"Yes, they are the complaining parties. Do I have to arrest you and toss you in jail for a few days?"

"Probably. Get Eagleton and Hendricks over here. I want them to accuse me face to face!"

"Reasonable." Spur called to the other two men to come over and talk. They were hesitant.

Hendricks stopped beside Spur. "Sure you got his gun? He's a sneaky old bastard."

"Hendricks, why did you shoot me?" Scotty asked.

"Two of my beef died today, no water. That's why."

Scotty turned half over where he lay on the ground, pulled a derringer and fired. The round smashed into Hendrick's leg and he bellowed in rage.

As soon as he saw the small gun, Spur dove at Scotty. He arrived just after the round ripped out of the barrel. He knocked the weapon out of Scotty's hand and grabbed it. He patted the smaller man down and made sure he had no more weapons.

"Now, you god-damned trio of jackasses. We're going to sit down and not move until we work out this problem. There is going to be no more shooting. Is that clear?"

Spur boomed the ultimatum at them in his best parade ground angry officer voice. All three wilted. For the first time, they realized that one or more of them could have been killed.

"You three don't look this stupid. You know right now I could arrest both of you on attempted murder charges. What would happen to your ranches while you sat in jail waiting for the trial? And then, if convicted, and with my testimony you damn well would be, you would get from three to five years in the Kansas State Prison. How does that sit with you?"

He waited for two minutes, letting them think it over.

"Fine. Now I'll tell you what is going to happen here. Scotty, you've got a fine dry lake bed here. You're right to use it to save water for a dry spell. But you can't save all the water. I'll mark the stream and show you where you can put in a diversion gate. Then you can divert one third of the water coming downstream and put it in the lake."

"Then he can't water his stock below, right?" Eagleton asked.

"Correct, Mr. Eagleton. According to the irrigation and water rights law, each of you has rights to one third of the runoff water. Is that perfectly clear?"

"No, damnit!" Scotty said. "How can I tell if I get all of my rightful one third?"

Spur helped him stand and showed him the stream. Spur stepped on rocks and then into the foot deep stream. "Right about here you drive in a stake. It's one third of the way across and the current is about the same all the way. You put your wooden diversion gate in here at an angle so it doesn't pile up the water.

"One third of the stream goes into your lake. The rest goes downstream. If your lake gets full, and there's plenty of water, you lift your diversion gate and let it all flow downstream. Clear?"

"Yeah. Damn, I hate these modern times. Like the

old days better.''

"We get to inspect the gate? Check his lake?'' Hendricks asked.

"Yes,'' Spur ruled. "Anytime these gentlemen wish to inspect the gate and your lake, you must grant them free access to the area.''

"Hell, okay, okay. I understand. Now will somebody help me get back on my horse so I can ride to my place?''

They helped Scotty on his mount.

"One more thing, Mr. MacDougal. Your diversion ditch has been in place for about thirty days, I understand. You are enjoined from putting in your diversion gate for 60 days, to allow the downstream ranches their fair share of the past 30 days of water.''

"Hell, you got anymore surprises for me?''

"One more. I'm filing attempted murder charges against both of you with the sheriff and leaving my legal deposition, detailing what happened. If either of you go back on this agreement, or violate the water rights in any way, these charges will be brought against both of you and you'll have to stand trial. In my business I call this a little insurance that you'll behave yourselves like adults.''

Scotty rode off, mumbling to himself.

Hendricks scowled as he watched Spur. "That true about the attempted murder charge?''

"Absolutely. You fired first, I should just charge you, but this way I have a hold over Scotty as well. Now both of you grow up and start acting like adults.''

They rode back just as the low sun started to

throw long shadows. Spur knew it would be dark before he got back to town. They dropped off Hendricks at his ranch and Eagleton invited him to stop by his place for supper. It was almost time.

Spur decided he might as well. The ranch house was smaller than he guessed. Eagleton said he'd only been there four years and was just starting to build up a good herd. He should have a thousand herd for sale later in the summer.

He met Mrs. Eagleton, a small woman who had gone to fat at forty, and their twenty-year-old daughter, Alice. She came in only when supper was ready, ate with no comments and glanced up at Spur only once. She smiled shyly, then looked away.

They had pheasant and rice and potatoes and vegetables with lots of homemade bread and fresh butter. The coffee was boiled to death but tasted good. Spur ate too much, then thanked Mrs. Eagleton who beamed.

"I love to see a man eat!" she told him as he was leaving.

A quarter of a mile down the road to town, Spur realized someone was coming up behind him. He stopped and looked back, wondering if he had forgotten his rifle or his hat. He hadn't.

A moment later a black horse materialized out of the darkness with Alice on board. She smiled and rode up until their legs almost touched.

"I wanted to thank you for having supper with us. We don't get many visitors."

"Quite all right, Miss Alice."

She hesitated. "Mr. Smith, would you kiss me? I don't get much chance to practice my kissing."

Spur laughed. "Might be arranged."

"Right here?" she asked. He nodded. She pushed her horse closer and leaned toward him. A moment later she fell off the horse and he caught her. One of his hands came to rest around her ample right breast.

She looked up at him and smiled. "Thanks for catching me, maybe we better try kissing off our horses."

Alice kicked off the mount and slid to the ground. Spur dropped beside her and she caught his hand and led him to the side of the trail where some fresh spring grass grew. She sat down and he sat beside her.

"Now, the kiss."

He bent toward her and her arms went around him locking fast. Her lips found his and then her teeth caught his lower lip and held on. She pressed hard against him. When she let loose with her teeth, she smiled and kissed his lips and his nose and then both of his eyes.

"I knew at supper I just had to fuck you. Would you mind? I just have to feel you big and hard inside my little cunny."

"Now this is a surprise," Spur said. "You barely looked at me at supper."

"I was busy rubbing myself under the table," she said. She pulled open her blouse and her breasts tumbled out, restricted by no other garment. "Please kiss them!"

Spur didn't need a second invitation. Her milky white breasts had small areolas and thumb sized nipples. Her hands found his crotch and tore at the fly buttons until they were open. She probed inside his pants with her hands, and squealed in joy when she pulled free his erection.

"Oh, wonderful!" she said. She dropped between his legs, sucking all of his shaft into her mouth, chewing him, pulling, then starting an up and down motion with her head that set him on fire.

A dozen strokes later, Spur exploded with a moan as he spurted his load into her willing mouth and she made small, happy noises as she sucked every drop from his planting tool. Slowly she came away from him. She kissed him.

"Did you like me doing you that way?"

"Oh, yes!"

"Good, now you do me!" She caught his head and pulled it down to her crotch. She pawed at her skirt and petticoats pulling them up over her chest. She wore thin drawers.

"Bite through the cloth over my cunny!" she ordered. Spur bent and bit the cloth, tearing it. He used his hands to tear more of it, then smelled her musk.

He kissed around her soft pubic hair, then her hands caught his head and pressed him forward to her heartland.

He was there. He kissed the pink lips, then licked them and she began to climax over him. He licked her and kissed her outer lips until she erupted in a grinding, moaning and flailing mass of arms and legs as she exploded around him.

She shook and vibrated and spasm after spasm tore into her body. Alice's breath came in great gulps to keep her alive and her whole body gyrated and shivered and her hips humped against his face until the climax paled and she lay in the grass panting and wheezing.

When her breathing quieted, he lay next to her and looked over at the shy ranch girl.

"My God! Are you still alive?"

"Barely. You were beautiful!"

"Is it always so wild for you?"

"Oh yes, especially when you go down below that way. I go wild for a few minutes."

"Your father know you're out here?"

"No! He'd shit his pants. Mom knows. She said she fooled around every chance she got starting about sixteen. She got pregnant when she was nineteen and then got married. I figure I can fuck for another year before somebody gets me with a kid. Plenty of time to get married then."

She rolled quickly on top of him and pumped her hips at his crotch. "Once more?"

Spur shook his head, kissed her and buttoned up his pants.

"You would kill me for sure if I tried again. Right now I have to get on my horse and get back to town."

"Can you come back out?"

"Probably not. I have some business in town."

"Jeeze you were good. It's been three months for me. I was ready."

"You certainly were."

They stood up and she arranged her clothes, then pulled Spur's hands inside her blouse.

"Sure you can't stay for one more?"

He kissed her and took his hands away.

"I'm sure." He helped her mount her horse, then swung up himself.

"One more kiss, and I promise not to fall off. That was all an act."

"I know." He kissed her, then rode away. When he looked back she was watching him and waving.

Spur rode hard for town then. He got back slightly before 8:30 and went straight to the sheriff's office. He told Sheriff Johnson what happened and about the attempted murder charges. He filled out a form, and then wrote up the charges, dated it and left it all with the sheriff.

"Now, has anything happened here?" Spur asked.

"Quiet as a grave," the sheriff said.

"You don't quite take this threat seriously, do you, Johnson?"

"Damn right I do, but I'm not going to let it make me into a recluse crying and whining all day long."

"Good. When do you get locked up?"

"Ten o'clock. I've been inside here since it got dark."

"Any good suspicious characters hanging around town waiting for it to get dark?"

"A few. There are always suspicious characters here in Dodge. You just have to take your pick."

"That's a lot of help. Everything quiet?"

"So far."

"What cell will you be in?"

"First one. It's closer to the outhouse."

Spur waved and headed out the door. He'd make a round of the saloons. Maybe he could turn up something interesting.

He did on the second stop. The kid's name was

Verner Archer. He was the top sheet on the list of flyers sent out. Verner had been wanted by the sheriff in Greensburg for murder and bank robbery.

Spur loosened his gun in the leather, and moved into the shadows of the saloon as he settled in to watch every move that Archer made. He might have his sights on the lawman killer. He damn sure wasn't going to let Archer slip through his fingers. One way or another, Archer was finished!

10

Vern Archer tipped the mug of beer and drank. A chill settled over him and he let the beer down slowly. He kept both hands on top of the bar.

Somebody was watching him. He'd felt it before. Once it happened just before some bushwhacker put a slug through his lung and almost killed him out of Tucson. Never was going to let that happen again.

He turned with his beer to watch the poker players, and as he did he surveyed the whole saloon, casually, not making it obvious.

Arthur saw no one he knew, nobody who looked like a lawman. He eased back to the bar and put his boot up on the brass rail. Maybe he was getting jumpy. He had a job to do in town and he would stay here until it was done. Nothing was going to change that. Once he made up his mind he was as bull-headed as an old buffalo charging down a line of flight. Nothing but death could budge him off that selected course.

He finished the beer, stood next to a poker game for a while, then meandered toward the saloon's front door. He hadn't lived this long by his wits and his .44 to get cut down from a dark alley by some bounty hunter or do-gooder. Not by a damn sight!

Archer walked through the front door of the saloon, then jumped to the street and sprinted silently for the closest alley. He got there two stores down on the same side of the street and edged into the blackness.

Automatically, he pulled the .44 from his hip and and held it ready, the heavy hammer cocked and ready. A man came out of the swinging doors of the same saloon he had just left, looked both ways, then ambled toward the hotel. Two more men came out laughing and telling bawdy stories. Three more men came out and left in various directions.

Archer pushed his six-gun back in leather. He rubbed the back of his neck with his right hand and frowned. Maybe the strain was telling on him. Maybe he should give it up and forget old angers and move on west somewhere, out of the hellhole of Kansas.

Vern Archer shook his head standing there in the dark. Damn no! He came to town to do a job and he fucking well was going to do it! He stomped up on the boardwalk and stalked back to the saloon he had just left.

If anybody wanted him, they would have to face him down in the lamplight of the saloon. That way he'd have a fair chance. And lately he'd been as good as anybody he'd met with a gun. Better, in fact, because he was still alive and several of the others weren't.

Spur McCoy had eased out of the saloon behind

two other men and wandered across the street. He faded into some shadows of a farm wagon and watched the area around the drinking and gambling establishment. Archer was out there somewhere.

Five minutes later, someone came from the alley two doors down from the saloon, looked around, then walked determinedly back to the card room and bar. In a flash of light at the door, Spur saw that the man was Vern Archer. He'd been scared by something and went outside to watch and wait.

Nobody was better at waiting than Spur McCoy. He eased his hat down a notch over his eyes and went back in the saloon. The Secret Service Agent picked up a beer at the bar and wandered around the poker tables, asking if he could sit in at tables that were full. He got waved away.

After moving halfway around the room, he spotted Archer again. He had joined a poker game at one of the dollar limit tables. Archer had never been a big gambler.

Spur leaned against the wall, sipped on his beer and watched the players and the three chippies who sold drinks as they bent over a lot to show off swinging breasts and round bottoms. One of the girls squealed and slapped a cowboy who got his hand under her skirt and rubbed her crotch.

She yelped but didn't move, knowing what she was doing. A minute later she kissed him, caught his arm and pulled him to the door that led to the cribs in back. His buddies at the table hooted him on and he couldn't turn back. The girl was a great little salesman.

Spur made sure Archer was still at the poker

table. He was losing. Spur didn't want simply to arrest Archer on an old charge. That was too easy. If Archer was the lawman killer, he wanted to catch him in the act—almost. It would be perfect to nail him just as he grabbed the sheriff, but before he had a chance to use his hideout derringer.

Yeah, but it wouldn't happen that way because Sheriff Johnson was safely locked up in his own jail. That was a problem, but if Archer was the serial killer, he'd figure out a way to get the sheriff out long enough to kill him. Spur had to be sitting there waiting for Archer's move and nail the bastard.

A half hour later, Spur began to feel obvious and self-conscious in his position. He sat in on a poker game where he could look at Archer's back. It was a quarter limit table, and using half of his attention, he won six dollars in the first four hands. Then he lost two by throwing in his hands on a five card draw.

When he checked Archer after the hand was over, the outlaw stood, scooped some change into his hat and headed for the door. Spur quit his game, left two dollars in the pot as compensation for his winnings, and left the saloon a few seconds after Archer. Another man went out the same time Spur did.

Archer was ahead of him, moving toward a cheap hotel. From the street, Spur watched him go inside, talk with the room clerk a minute, then slip him some money and examine the register. The man didn't live there, but he was interested in who did.

When Archer headed out the front door, Spur walked slowly toward the main part of town.

Wrong choice.

When Archer came out he headed the other way. He walked quickly now along the dirt streets, checking houses from time to time. He stopped in front of one that still had lights on. It was a modest frame structure, five or six rooms, one story, with a small picket fence around the front that had been whitewashed. There were even some flowers in the yard and two trimmed lilac bushes flourished.

He stood at the gate a moment, then he mumbled something, kicked the gate and spun on his boot and headed back toward town. Spur slid down a cross street and waited for his target to pass, then followed.

Vern Archer rushed into the first saloon he came to. It was the smallest one in town, had no girls and no poker games. It was for drinkers. He ordered three draft beers and drank them all before the head bubbled away on the last one.

Spur watched him through the window. Archer pulled his pistol and fired three times into the ceiling, then lurched out of the saloon, nearly knocking Spur down as the lawman had been charging inside.

Archer swore at him without seeing who he was, and continued down the boardwalk. Spur followed.

Half a block down, Archer saw something and waited in the shadows. A deputy sheriff walked his rounds, checking each merchant's front door along the boardwalk. Archer crouched behind a rain barrel in the darkness of the alley and waited. The deputy came closer.

In the moonlight, Spur saw Archer's six-gun come up as the deputy turned from the dry goods shop and walked forward.

"Look out, Deputy!" Spur bellowed. It was enough to make the lawman jump to the side. Archer's aim followed and he fired once. The round slammed through the deputy's side and dumped him on the boardwalk.

By that time Spur had sent two rounds at the shadow near the water barrel. Archer vanished down the alley away from main street and Spur charged forward. He checked the deputy.

"How bad are you hit?" Spur asked.

The deputy held his own pistol and recognized Spur. "Not bad, go get the bastard!"

Spur sprinted down the alley heard movement ahead and dove flat in the dirt as two rounds whispered three feet over his prone body. He saw the flashes ahead and fired twice, heard a gasp and then swearing as footsteps sounded out the other end of the alley.

Spur ran again. At the alley mouth he saw a street. Only a few businesses and a few houses. He saw no movement. Then from the side of the closest house he heard a horse snorting. McCoy charged across the street, down to the house and along the side of it until he could see a small shed at the back.

As he checked it, he heard more movement, and a rider raced from the shed on board a dark horse. Spur got off two shots at the rapidly vanishing target, then ran to the shed. One more horse stood there pawing the stall.

Spur grabbed a bridal and threw it over the horses' head, pushed the bit into the animal's mouth and vaulted on board bareback. He pulled the horse's head around and kicked it in the flanks.

For a moment Spur almost lost his seat as the animal spurted away after its stablemate.

Spur could still see the dim form of a rider pounding out the street that almost at once ended in the prairie. He stopped a moment and listened. There were faint sounds from ahead as the animal hit a harder spot and hoofbeats drifted back.

Spur rode again.

A half hour later he lost the trail where Archer had splashed through a small stream and come out on a hard rocky slope. He could have angled either way from there.

Nothing to do but stop and wait for dawn, which was then about five hours away.

Vern Archer could be half way to Wichita by dawn. Spur reconsidered. Archer could not make it quite that far, but with a good horse a five hour start could mean at least a twenty mile head start. If he kept going. He might stop and light a fire and go to sleep.

Spur snorted. Not Vern Archer. He had come out of the war and simply never stopped fighting the North. Nothing he loved more than a good fight, especially with some "damn bluebellies." Half the lawmen in the West knew Vern Archer. Catching him was another problem.

Several bits of evidence pointed toward Archer as the lawman killer. He was Southern, hated all Northerners. He had been arrested before by one of the dead lawmen, he had taken an unprovoked shot at a deputy who he could have mistaken for the sheriff.

A damn good suspect, Spur decided. Especially since right now Archer was the only suspect he had.

He put the horse on a long lead line to graze and settled down against a tree for some sleep. He had half convinced himself that Archer was not taking off for Denver or St. Louis. He must have come to town for a purpose, like killing Sheriff Johnson. That could mean Archer would make a wide circle and be back in town long before Spur could follow his tracks.

McCoy quit trying to second guess the outlaw and instructed his subconscious to wake him slightly before dawn. Then he went to sleep.

Spur was up and moving with the first streaks of light. He picked up the freshest tracks off the slabs of rock and found the outlaw had not turned back toward the city. Spur also found some drops of blood on the slick rock surface. His slugs had made contact with flesh and Archer must be hurting.

Would Archer go to ground or run? Head back to town later for some medical work, or gut it out with some homemade bandages out of his own shirt? He had no supplies for a long ride. There was little chance to live off the land out here in the Kansas prairie. Not even many ranches or farms to stop at for a friendly handout.

Spur worked his fast tracking technique. He judged where the trail would go, and rode quickly ahead to a pre-determined point or a half mile, and got off and inspected the ground for the continuing tracks. This worked best when a rider was lighting out for a long run over known terrain.

Here it was risky, but once the trail was lost, it

only involved backtracking to the last known point and working the tracks on foot.

Spur won the bet on the first three half mile contents, then the trail vanished. He went back to the small cottonwood near the bend in the creek where Archer had cut across. From there he looked all around. Slightly rolling ground, mostly flat. He stared each direction and then caught the first whiff of a fire. Campfire or wood stove?

He rode in a two hundred yard circle around the last spotted Archer hoofprints, and found the trail angling back toward town. It turned again, followed down a small draw and across an almost dry creek. A quarter of a mile down, Spur saw a cabin.

It was what was left of what had been a small farm. One cow still munched where she was tied to a stake near the stream. Smoke came slowly from the chimney. The house was no more than twelve by twelve. It was the kind with "minimum improvements" that had to be made on a homestead to "prove it up" and gain title.

Somebody was home.

Spur moved up on the cabin along the brush line of the creek. He left his horse two hundred yards from the cabin and rushed across an open space between trees and brush on the creek. He was halfway across when a rifle snarled from the back window of the cabin.

The slug dug up dirt at his feet and Spur darted the last ten feet before the gunman could aim and fire again.

Spotted.

Was Archer alone in the cabin or was there a

hostage?

The creek ran within twenty feet of the front of the cabin. As he got closer through the now denser brush, he could see that the place was occupied. A washstand had been built near the creek, and a string of pots hung in the sun on the back cabin wall. An axe stuck in a chopping block and two arm-loads of split wood lay nearby.

There was only one outbuilding, a shameful excuse for a barn. Evidently the cow would not live in it. Both the front poles that held up the roof were leaning to the left. The roof of shingles was in drastic need of repair.

Spur found a log, crawled behind it and lifted his hat just barely over the top of the log with a stick. A rifle bullet slammed into his hat, spinning it off the stick and ten yards away. He retrieved it without danger. So Archer had found a rifle inside. Who else was in there?

The Secret Service Agent edged through the brush again until he could see the front door. He sent one .45 round into the side of the frame house. There was no response.

What next? He had an idea, reversed his direction and got into the barn with only a short dash across ten yards of open space. He found the same horse he had seen charge away from the shed in Dodge last night. It still had its saddle on. Spur cinched the saddle, and rode out of the barn and behind the brush screen for a hundred yards upstream where he tied up the mount and jogged back to the barn.

He found some interesting items he might be able to use to smoke the killer out of the cabin without endangering anyone inside.

Spur checked again. Yes, the back side of the cabin had no window. It faced the excuse for a barn. Spur carried the heavy sheet of tin and a half dozen burlap gunny sacks as he ran from the barn to the back of the cabin. He went up the low back wall which had been dug three feet into the edge of a small slope and was soon on the roof.

Smoke came freely from the chimney now. The hostage could be cooking food for Archer. McCoy put the tin over the chimney and then bound the six gunny sacks over the tin to stop up the flue. He made sure the sacks were secure and looked over the front of the roof to see who would come out of the smoke choked cabin first.

They held out for nearly five minutes, then Archer came out, a wet cloth over his nose, and a woman clamped tightly to his chest with one arm as he backed away. He dropped the cloth once out in the open and drew his .44. Spur saw the bloody bandage on his left arm. The arm would need medical attention.

Archer's big gun touched the woman's head.

"Whoever you are, one wrong move and this lady gets her head blown off. You want that?"

"Go ahead, I don't even know who she is. You kill her and your shield is useless. I'd bet you won't do that, it's just a bluff."

Archer kept backing toward the barn.

"Might be a bluff, but you ain't shooting."

"Your horse isn't there. I know who you are. There isn't another horse there either. You might as well give up."

"Not while I'm breathing, whoever you are. I come to Dodge to do me a job, and I'm gonna do it. You stay outa my way, or I'll start my work by killing this woman and you."

"Big talker with a small brain," Spur snarled. "You got about one chance in a dozen of finding your horse before I ride you down and ventilate your worthless hide with six .45 rounds."

Archer kept backing up, heading for the brush. He was soon there and pulled the woman into it with him, then dropped her and ran north, upstream toward where Spur had hidden his horse. He would find it.

Spur leaped off the back of the house and hurried inside, he located the rifle, saw that it was functioning. A single shot carbine. He grabbed a dozen cartridges and took the rifle as he raced out the door toward the horse upstream. If he was lucky he could get there in time to kill the horse. Then he would have Archer on foot and a much easier quarry.

All he needed now was enough time and a little luck. He also would be thankful if Archer didn't figure out what his opponent in this little chess game might do.

Spur came around the barn and found Archer standing there waiting for him, the six-gun already up in a two-handed firing position. Spur heard the gun go off as he pulled up the just borrowed rifle.

11

The booming report of the six-gun overlapped a sudden jolting force as the slug smashed into the wooden stock of the carbine. The stock slammed into Spur's shoulder and powered him backward.

It happened in slow motion then for Spur McCoy. He was closer to death than he had been in a long time. He saw Archer thumbing back the hammer on his .44. Spur pivoted and tried to change directions in mid-air as he dove for the edge of the barn.

A slug thunked into the side of the barn and then McCoy was around the corner with the hard wood protecting him. He rolled to his feet and crouched at the edge of the barn, his Colt .45 in his hand.

He saw only a flash of green shirt as Archer ran into the heavy brush just beyond the barn. Spur sent three shots at him, paused to reload, putting in four rounds to load up with six in the cylinder.

Spur knew he had been damned lucky at the barn. The .44 slug from Archer should have gone through his chest where the outlaw had aimed. It had been mere chance when he moved up the rifle at exactly the right second and in precisely the right place to stop the death bringing bullet. That kind of luck ran out sooner or later.

Now he knew what he had to do. The rifle could misfire after the jolt it had taken. He couldn't chance it. He still had to get to the outlaw's horse before Archer found it. Spur had the advantage. He knew exactly where it was hidden.

The Secret Service Agent ran from the protection of the barn and into the virgin meadow that was well over a hundred yards wide. In the middle of the open space he turned and ran north, up stream. Even if Archer saw him he didn't have a weapon with enough range to reach him. Speed was the most essential right now.

Spur picked up his pace, holding the revolver in his right hand and pumping his arms. He had run a lot of foot races at Harvard, but never anything with boots on. Still he figured he was making good time.

At the spot where he had tied the mount, he turned and ran directly at the woods, his .45 leveled in front of him. Now was the critical point. If Archer stood just inside the cover behind a tree waiting for him, the chase would be over, and so would his life.

He tensed as he came closer. At twenty yards from the brush, he dodged one way and then the other to present a tougher target, and stormed forward.

It was almost a surprise when he swept into the brush and trees without being shot. Quickly he changed directions to get within ten yards of the horse, hunkered down behind an old willow and waited.

He heard Archer coming before he saw him. The man was jogging along, crashing through the brush, not trying to be quiet and watching behind him. He had stayed to the cover of the woods which meant slower going. Evidently he had no thought that Spur would dare move in the open ground.

Wait. Wait. Just like a military operation when you had the enemy walking into a trap. You had to wait for the right moment to spring it.

Archer was twenty yards from the horse. Now he saw it. He looked along his back trail and then ran forward. When he was less than five yards from Spur, the Agent leaned around the tree and cocked his pistol.

"Take another step, Archer, and you're breakfast for the buzzards!"

"Bastard!" Archer screamed. He let his .44 swing down, pointing at the ground and his shoulders slumped. Spur relaxed for a fraction of a second, and the outlaw sensed it. He angled up the six-gun and blasted a shot as he dove to the side and rolled into a smattering of small brush and a thicket of two inch trees.

Spur leaned out and fired three times. He saw two of the slugs bore into the small trees and the third hit a twig and whine away off target.

By then Archer had crawled to a substantial cottonwood tree that protected him.

"I'd say we have a standoff, lawman. Nobody else would know my name. You must have seen my advertising."

"The wanted posters. Lots of people have seen

them. How many men have you killed now, twelve or thirteen?"

"You're way behind the times, lawman. I hope you try for the horse."

"I'm in no hurry and you're not known for your patience."

"Don't matter, lawman. I got cover. I can get out of here and you'll never see me. But you're pinned down." Archer sent a slug zapping into Spur's willow tree.

"How many lawmen you killed now, Archer?"

"Who can count that high." He laughed. "Actually just one, beginner's luck about ten years ago. But I was fresh out of the Army, what did I know?"

Spur was figuring the odds. The gunman wouldn't miss if Spur made a surge for the horse. That was out. He didn't believe Archer's account of killed lawmen. He would never admit he was the serial killer.

Spur tried to breath softly so he could hear any movement by the outlaw ten yards away.

A meadowlark sang through his call in the edge of the grass. Spur heard nothing from Archer. The morning breeze rustled the tree leaves. No sound came from the outlaw.

Cat and mouse.

Was he there or not? There was no way to tell. Now Archer had the advantage. If he could make Spur think he had left and wait for a killing shot as the lawman moved, the game would all be over.

But, if Archer had left right after their last talk, he would be well on his way by now. No matter which guess was right, Spur McCoy knew he had to move.

Spur took a deep breath, picked out his first bit of protection, and dove to the left toward the horse. He rolled and stopped behind a decaying log that had fallen several years ago. It was barely a foot thick, but high enough.

There was no reaction from behind the cottonwood tree. Spur sucked in a pair of big breaths, then lifted up quickly with his eyes just over the log and stared at the cottonwood, then jerked his head down.

No shot. He was still alive. And he had not seen any sign of Archer behind the tree. The man could have moved around to the side to keep out of sight.

Somehow, Spur didn't think so. He was gone.

Spur checked his next burst. He had a dozen or so small trees growing five yards over. Not positive protection but it could be effective. He pulled his feet up under him, and surged to his feet and ran four long steps then dove to the ground behind the small trees, cradling the .45 to his chest but with the muzzle pointing away from his body.

No reaction.

He lifted up and stared at the cottonwood. The man was gone. He ran to the black with a saddle, untied her and stepped on board. Which way? Archer would stick to the screen of trees along the creek for cover. He would go downstream hoping to find Spur's horse. Then to the same little cabin.

Spur kicked the black into motion and charged through the brush into the meadow. There he raced upstream to where he had hidden his own mount.

The horse was still there. Good. He left the bareback horse there and rode back the way he had come toward the cabin. The woman who had been a hostage was still there. Her husband must have been on the range. The shots would have brought him back. Archer might have them both as hostages now if he went back to the cabin.

If he had gone back, it would be for food and the rifle, then he might run downstream to a ranch where he could steal a horse? Maybe.

As he rode easily, thinking about it, Spur heard three closely spaced pistol shots from downstream.

The signal for help, or to attract attention. Spur continued downstream toward the cabin. He came up around the same old barn and stayed out of sight as he dismounted and peered around the rotting siding.

Archer stood beside the door to the cabin. A man lay on the ground tied up. Archer held the same woman by the throat.

"Lawman, I know you're here somewhere. You make one bad move and the man here gets his head blown off. That clear? I know you can hear me."

Spur kept silent. Archer didn't know if his shots had pulled Spur back or not. He was playing a big bluff.

"You show yourself, lawman, or I'll start shooting these people in various, non fatal parts of their bodies."

Spur didn't respond.

"How about a nice little rape, you like that, lawman?" Archer caught the neck of the woman's dress and jerked downward. Her head snapped forward, then the cloth tore and seams parted and the whole front of her dress ripped to her waist. She wore only a thin petticoat top under the dess and now her breasts showed plainly. She tried to turn away. Arthur held her.

"Like that, lawman?"

Spur lay behind the barn and judged the distance. Almost forty yards. Too damn far! He needed another ten yards closer.

He hefted the Colt .45 with the ten-inch barrel and studied the scene again. If Archer stood to one side, there was a chance. His variation on longer shots was always up and down, never from side to side.

Spur brought up the .45 and steadied the long barrel on the pier block supporting the barn. He sighted in on Archer who had moved in front of the woman again and this time ripped off her petticoat top so her breasts were bare.

"Stop it!" the woman screamed.

Archer laughed.

"Women, they always want to get fucked, always beg for it. But most of them have a funny way of showing it." He stepped to one side, holding the woman by the wrist. "Look at her, lawman. Hell, you can have a turn after I leave. Just show yourself and lay down your iron and promise me you won't follow me."

Spur steadied the .45, aimed and made a slight elevation angle for the distance. He had only one chance, then the man would be dead and probably the woman too.

McCoy wiped sweat out of his eyes, and sighted in again. He aimed at the top of Archer's head, hoping that would be enough elevation to carry the slug into his chest.

"I can't wait all day. My old whip is getting hard as a baseball bat."

Spur fired. He could almost see the .45 slug fly through the air. A moment later Archer went down, clutching his right shoulder. The .44 in his right hand spun away and he moved toward it, away from the woman.

Spur fired twice more, then jumped around the barn and ran forward. One of Spur's shots had hit Archer in the belly. He tried to hold his shoulder now as he crawled toward his weapon. Spur fired at the six-gun but missed.

"Don't do it!" Spur bellowed.

"Hell, I'm a dead man either way." Archer crawled another two feet forward and looked at McCoy.

"Who the hell are you, anyway?"

"Spur McCoy, United States Secret Service."

"Figures. You weren't even looking for me, were you?"

"No. Have you been killing off the sheriffs down the stage line between here and Wichita?"

"Lawmen? Hell, no. I told you. Just that one when I was a fuzzy cheeked kid." He lunged for the weapon.

Spur fired again, the slug caught Archer in the side and angled downward into his gut. He screamed, tried to crawl forward, then held his belly.

Spur ran up and grabbed the six-gun off the ground and cut the cabin owner loose from his rope bounds. The man thanked Spur and hurried his hysterical wife into the cabin.

Spur sat on the grass beside Archer. The man was dying. There was no way to save him. The shot in the belly would do it in half an hour.

"Archer, you use a derringer?"

"Not usually. Don't own one."

"Did you just come from Greensburg?"

"Hell, no!" He cringed in pain. His face red. He screamed and screeched as the agony flooded through his whole body. Sweat beaded his forehead where he sat. Slowly he lay on his back.

The wave of hurt swept by and he shook his head. His anger came back. "Hell, no! I came here from McCook, Nebraska. There's a bank clerk up there who will testify to that. Still got most of the money in my hotel back in Dodge."

"Which one?"

"Dodge House. Under the name of Art Luther."

"I'll check it out. You know nothing about these lawmen killings?"

"Swear to God. Sounds like a good idea, but I'd rather just rob banks."

The lean, tall man came out of the cabin. He had the rifle, and a pistol.

"You need any help, I'll be more than willing," the man said.

"Thanks. Mr. Archer here is under control." The man went back inside. Soon smoke began to come from the chimney which had been cleared of its tin and burlap.

Archer doubled up in a spasm of pain, then stretched out swearing softly.

He looked up at Spur. "I'm dying, right? No way I

can live gut shot this way."

"Happens," Spur said. "You figured some day you'd go out this way, didn't you?"

- "Never did. Never thought about that. Just wanted to get more money to spend and enjoy life."

"That part's about over."

"Maybe half an hour," Archer said. He blinked tears out of his eyes. "Damn! I haven't cried since I was ten. Came here to see my wife. She left me a year ago. Lives in Dodge. Never quite got up nerve enough to go talk to her."

"That where you went last night to that little house with the picket fence?"

"Yeah. You were following me even then?"

"True. You're a famous man."

He saw the woman come from the cabin. She had put on a different dress and carried a cup. She walked up to Spur and looked down at Archer.

"Would a cup of coffee help, or some whiskey?"

Spur shook his head. "Not with a wound in the belly, ma'am, but thanks."

"Yeah, I'd like some whiskey," Archer said. "Is it going to ruin my health? You got any good whiskey, lady?"

She nodded and went back to the cabin.

Spur stared at Archer. "Drinking something now will only speed up the end."

"I'm not complaining. I'd do it quick if you'd give me my six-gun and one round. But don't reckon you will do that."

"Don't reckon."

They looked at each other. Archer coughed, spit up blood and shook as another round of killing pains raced through his belly and out into every nerve ending in his body. He rode through it, then wiped sweat off his brow.

The woman came back with a bottle of whiskey and a cup. She poured the cup half full and gave it to Spur.

"You sure, Archer?"

He nodded. "Damn right. Last things I want is a good drink of whiskey and to watch a pretty woman. Ma'am, sorry about the way I tore your dress. Would you sit and let me look at you? I never knew many nice women."

She frowned a minute, looked back at the cabin, then sat sedately in the grass a few feet from Spur.

"My name is Lucinda," she said.

"Verner, ma'am," he said.

He lifted the cup and smiled at her, then drank. When the whiskey went down his throat it made him cough, and that set up another spasm as the terrible pains marched through his body like Sherman heading for the sea.

Archer started to swear, then looked over at Lucinda.

"Sorry, ma'am, a bad habit."

Lucinda's husband came out of the cabin with the rifle that had saved Spur's life. He watched the little scene, then sat down leaning against the cabin.

"You want me to notify any kin, Archer?" Spur asked.

"Most don't have no truck with me." Archer looked up. "Might tell my wife and my sister. She's up in Omaha. She understood me best of any. Her name and street is in my gear." His face twisted as the pains came again, engulfing him. "Oh, lord! Sweet Jesus!"

"Yes, Verner! Yes, pray to Jesus!" Lucinda said softly. "He'll help you. He'll lift up your soul for an eternal home in paradise. Pray to him, Verner, and everything will be glorious!"

She was on her knees now, hands folded, eyes closed, praying silently.

Vern Archer looked at her in surprise. He frowned for a moment, then the pain touched him and he lifted up from the ground as the billowing fire burned higher and higher until it reached his brain, then he slumped back down.

Verner Archer had ceased to exist.

An hour later, Spur McCoy had tied Archer across the back of the bareback horse, said goodbye to the couple at the cabin and ridden out for Dodge. It would be only a two hour ride back to town.

12

Spur rode directly to the back door of the under-takers and gave him the body. There was no need to cause a stir on Main Street with a dead body. Then he went and talked with the sheriff.

"So you don't think this Vern Archer is the lawman killer? Why not? He tried to do in my deputy." Sheriff Johnson stared at Spur with a troubled frown.

"We talked about that. He'd been down the street to go visit his wife, lost his nerve and went back and finished getting drunk. He was mad at the whole world, and deputy sheriffs are not high on his favorite people list. He shot him in a stupid, drunken rage."

"Maybe so, maybe so. At least he was a wanted man. Wanted for two killings and about a dozen bank jobs. I'll send out a flyer that he's been disposed of so all those sheriffs can clean out their wanted drawer of him."

"You also get to tell his wife that he's dead, which won't be bad news for her, from what he said. He also told me there's some McCook, Nebraska, bank robbery money in his room at the hotel under the name I told you."

"Yeah, we'll clean out his room, give his personal effects to his wife. Except the cash from the bank. that will go back to McCook, Nebraska."

Sheriff Johnson eased into his big chair behind his desk and leaned forward toward Spur.

"You think the killer is still in town? I was hoping like blazes that you had him on the run last night."

"He's still here. Just waiting his chance. This is a smart one, willing to wait. How long has it been now since Greensburg, six, seven days? He's in no rush."

"That gives him the advanrage."

"The man on the attack always has an advantage over the defensive position. You never know when he's coming, and he times his attack on you at the worst possible moment for you. We just have to stay calm, play it right and stay alert."

"Besides that, I get locked in a cell every night."

"Good for you. Maybe you'll put better mattresses in there for your guests."

Spur moved toward the door. "Next on my list is food. I missed breakfast and dinner. You look at Vern, fill out the paper and I'll sign it."

Spur ate and hurried upstairs. He wanted to change clothes, catch up on his sleep and be roaring ready when the sun went down to prowl Dodge City and nail the bastard who had been shooting all the lawmen. There had to be a familiar face here somewhere.

In the lobby he met Lila. He grinned and said hello, but she turned away and walked past him. She carried a big paper sack in her hands and headed up the stairs. He followed her a moment later, caught up with her on the steps up to the third floor.

"I thought I knew you, Miss. You look just like a beautiful singer I know called Lila. Maybe you aren't the same girl. I guess I was wrong."

She let a grin sparkle over her face before she frowned again.

"People who know Lila tell her when they are going to miss her performances. Somebody I know missed both of them last night."

They were at her door. She opened it and turned. "So?"

"I was out of town, getting shot at by a bank robber, and trying to figure out why I was there. Then I slept on the ground and was miserable and cold and wishing I had you to keep warm beside."

"Good, I hoped it was something like that."

A couple passed them in the hallway and went down the steps.

She stepped into her room, reached out and pulled him in by one arm, then closed her door. A second later she had her arms around him hugging him tightly and looking upward to be kissed.

Spur answered the request.

"Now, that's better," she said. Lila pointed at the sack she had tossed on the bed. "I bought a new dress and I want you to help me try it on."

Spur kissed her again, then put one hand over one of her breasts.

"Does this involve some removal of your current costume?"

"Yes."

"Good, I like you half dressed, and then undressed and all bare assed naked."

"Mr. Smith! What a naughty thing to say! I'm shocked. I'd rather be fucked, but I'm shocked." She laughed. "Now help me get out of this dress so I can try on the new one."

"My second most favorite sport, watching a pretty lady take off her dress." He unbuttoned the fasteners in back of the dress and spun her around.

"When I'm not helping, how do you get these things buttoned and unbuttoned?"

She smiled as she lifted the dress off over her head. She had on the soft blue chemise. Her breasts were delightfully half hidden. He bent and kissed them.

"Darling, not right now. Be patient. About the buttons, I get them fastened with a lot of swearing and stretching. Usually I don't buy dresses that fasten that way."

She stroked one hand up his crotch and felt the growing lump there.

"My, my, we are excitable today, aren't we?" She lifted one brow and smiled at him. "Poor baby has to wait." She took the new dress out of the box and held it up to her chest.

"Well?"

"Nice, but it covers up too much of the lady behind it. I like the naked look."

"Good." She held the dress and then slipped it over her head mussing her hair. She fastened three snaps in the front and adjusted it to her satisfaction looking in the wavy mirror over the dresser. She turned. The dress was beautiful. It was much lower cut than the other and the top of the lace chemise showed.

"Yes, I'll have to use different undergarments. But what do you think?"

"Nice, extremely nice. Too good for these country cowboys at the saloon where you sing."

"Good, I didn't buy it for them, I bought it to impress you!"

She walked over slowly, put out her arms and held him, then kissed his offered lips. The kiss lasted a long time.

"I like the dress, but right now I'd rip it off you for half a penny."

"Don't you dare. It's time for my afternoon nap. I need a lot of sleep and working late I never get to sleep until after midnight."

"I'll have a nap with you."

She giggled. "Now that would be fun, but neither of us would get any sleep."

"The sexy part would be fun, though."

"Tonight, after work. I'm at the Silver Dollar. You be there for the last show at eleven and then we'll come back here and make love until neither of us has the strength to wiggle and you can't get it up anymore!"

"Done!" Spur said. "I'll get out of here. I can't stand to see you take that dress off. I might attack you."

"Please!" She giggled. "Only do it tonight."

Spur kissed her nose goodbye and went down to his room. There was a note under his door when he went inside. It was written on a school tablet paper with lines on it.

"Mr. Smith. I must see you. Come to 142 Second Street before dark."

Spur washed up, shaved and changed clothes. That was what he was headed to do before he saw Lila. Feeling back in civilized society again after his wash and shave, he walked out of the hotel and tried to remember where Second Street was.

After a block's walk down Main Street he found it. Spur strolled two more blocks and came to a small house with a white picket fence.

The new widow's house, he decided. This was where Archer had kicked the gate last night. If he'd gone inside he'd probably still be alive.

Spur saw the curtain move at the window. He was spotted. He walked through the gate up to the front door. It opened just as he was about to knock.

"Mr. Smith?" a tall, blonde woman asked. She was at least five feet eight and slender.

"Yes. You must be Mrs. Archer."

"I was at one time. I took my maiden name when I discovered Verner. I understand that you're the man who killed my ex-husband."

"Yes, ma'am. We had a gunfight."

"You must be good with a gun because Verner was one of the best."

She stared at him a minute, then opened the door. "Please come in, we have to talk."

"Archer tried to come see you last night, but he changed his mind and left. That's when he got drunk and shot the deputy sheriff."

"He always tries to see me when he comes to Dodge. I never let him in the door. He just wants to . . ." She sighed. "He just wants to have his way with me and then leave. I never let him in the house anymore."

"I didn't try to kill him, Mrs. Archer."

"Mrs. Grenville. I took back my maiden name."

"Yes, Mrs. Grenville. It just happened. Sometimes it's the other man or me who gets hurt."

"Oh, I'm not blaming you. It's just that. . . ." She stopped. "I made a vow to myself, two years ago. I promised myself that if somebody did kill Verner or put him in prison, I'd be . . . I'd be extra special nice to that man."

"Not necessary, ma'am. I'm a law officer, so this is just a part of my regular job."

Mrs. Grenville opened the top button on her dress and kept at it until they were free all the way to her waist.

"No, I insist. This is a debt I need to pay. I need to give myself to you, as payment, to meet my promise to myself. I won't let you say no." She shrugged out of her dress top showing proud breasts surging forward. The areolas were brown tipped with heavy brown nipples centering them. He could see the nipples full of hot blood and throbbing.

"I want you to understand, Mr. Smith. I'm not a loose woman. I have not given myself to a man since Verner last raped me about four years ago. That's a long time to wait. . . ." She shook her head. "I don't mean that. It's a long time to be without the love of a good man."

She caught his hand and brought it over one of her breasts, then found his other hand and led him through two rooms into her bedroom.

"My son won't be home until supper time. We

have three hours, and I want to pleasure you just every way you can think of." She paused. "Mr. Smith, you do like women, don't you?"

"Oh, yes, especially remarkably attractive women such as yourself."

"Then this . . . this arrangement . . . is agreeable to you?"

They sat down on the edge of the bed and he took her hand and placed it at the large lump extending up from his crotch.

She grinned. "Mr. Smith, I think this is going to work out just fine."

She slipped the dress off over her head and, to Spur's surprise, she wore nothing under it. She had been ready and waiting for him. She lay on the bed for a moment, her legs spread and her knees raised.

Spur watched her for a moment, then slipped out of his vest and by that time she was on her knees on the bed unbuttoning his shirt. His pants came next and when he was as naked as she was, she knelt on her hands and knees over him, letting her breasts swing down to his face.

"Eat them, Mr. Smith! Damn, I haven't done this, or said anything like that for six years! But the feeling is just the same: delightful, marvelous!"

Spur lay there still a little surprised. He'd seen gratitude before, but this was the best kind. This woman was everything that Lila wasn't. She was tall, full boned, slender, strongly built, with long legs and a delightful softly blonde muff and wide hips for easy childbirth.

This was not going to be a quick pop and out the door. Mrs. Grenville was settled in for a full afternoon of lovemaking. When he sucked and chewed on her second breast, she collapsed on top of him in a quick climax that sent her into shrieks of delight and a passionate kiss that left him drained. She ended the climax and lifted away from him.

She flipped on her back, spread her legs and urged him to come between them. Then she lifted them high in the air and placed her deliciously long and slender legs on his shoulders.

"Just once this way," she said softly. "You go in so deep I don't want you ever to come out!"

He did, amazed at the long legs over his shoulders and what she did with her internal muscles, gripping his shaft and letting go and then grabbing him again. She slowed him down, making him last longer than he thought was possible.

At last she nodded and began coming up with her hips to meet him and they both exploded almost at the same time. She screeched in rapture again and kept pumping long after he was through. She opened her eyes.

"Like that one? I've got about a dozen more to try if you can hold out. Maybe we should cut it down to six more. You look like about a seven fucker to me."

She ducked her head as she said the taboo word. She was away from him as soon as he moved to the side of the bed. She came back with three bottles of cold beer, a plate of small sandwiches and pickles.

"Most men get hungry and thirsty when they make love. I want this to be one you'll remember. I always will. Is five minutes enough between times?"

Spur nodded. The beer was cold, the sandwiches delicious and the woman amazing. It looked like it was going to be a damned interesting afternoon.

Dusk had fallen when he put on his clothes. Spur had to admit that he was not used to being a "seven timer" he knew that was a record for an afternoon of lovemaking. He grinned as he slipped on his boots. The woman had not dressed and lay there in a sexy, provocative pose.

"Figured you might like one last sexy look before you left," she said.

She watched him dress. "You don't want to get married, do you? We could do this every week, on Thursday. That way you'd keep your pistol clear and I'd be able to settle down a little and maybe relax."

Spur laughed softly.

"No, I figured not. You're not ready to get married, not yet. Maybe I'll take a lover, it's been known to happen. Find some nice young man who needs a woman and we could get together once a week or so."

"On Thursdays," Spur said.

She laughed, sat up, her big breasts bouncing. "Yeah, on Thursday. Fucking on Thursday!"

Mrs. Grenville saw him to the door, had him kiss both her breasts before he left. He stepped into the late afternoon dusk, not really sure how this all had happened, but realizing that he had helped Mrs. Grenville close out one phase of her life, and maybe launched her in a new and more fulfilling direction.

Spur checked in at the sheriff's office. Sheriff Johnson was just having his dinner off a tray from the Town House Cafe. He had been using a different eatery every day so he wouldn't make any of them mad.

"Quiet?"

"Too damn quiet. I'm getting the jitters. I bet you a two dollar gold piece we never see this lawman killer here in Dodge. He heard I was here and you were here and he just bypassed Dodge and headed on to Garden City, fifty miles or so on down the stage line."

"As soon as I see a kill report on the sheriff over there, I'll believe it," Spur said. He sniffed the plate of fried chicken in front of the sheriff. "Supper time for me, too. I'll be back tonight. Try and stay healthy."

The sheriff looked up. "Smith, I been thinking. This damn killer could make it yet. Somehow. But I got my mind made up about one thing. If some son-of-a-bitch does catch me and kills me dead, I'm gonna do my damnedest to tell you before I cash out of the game, just who it is.

"I don't know how, and maybe I can't. But if I do show up dead one of these days, you go over everything on or near me, because I'm sure as hell going to be trying to tell you something, even as I'm lying there bleeding to death."

"I hear you, Frank. But that's one problem I'm not going to have. I've seen enough lawmen die. I don't relish seeing any more go down. If I do my job here right, we won't have any more problems that way.

"Now, enough of this morbid talk. You haven't eaten half that plate of chicken yet. Dig in. I don't want to see the county wasting food."

Spur grinned and walked out of the sheriff's office, but he had a deadly feeling somewhere in his gut. He was sure now that he hadn't seen the last dead lawman. He hated the idea, but it was there and he couldn't make it go away, no matter how hard he tried.

13

McCoy left the sheriff's office and headed down the Dodge City street. The small town had shown a remarkable growth in only a few years. It was like a magnet for half the gamblers and gunsharps in the west. A lot of fast gun reputations had been made and lost here, and usually for nothing but the glory of it and the resulting blood.

He ducked into the biggest gambling house in town, a saloon called the Last Drink. It had a fifty foot long bar, over thirty gambling tables, and layouts for faro, monte, seven up and roulette.

Spur was still watching faces, checking the stage whenever he could, looking for that face or even a swing of the shoulders he had seen before in Greensburg and back down the bloody line of dead lawmen toward Wichita.

So far it had not produced any results.

He had a short beer, walked around the gambling tables and gave up. Maybe at the next saloon.

Spur would work his way toward the hotel and supper, but on the way he could check half a dozen saloons. Damn, the hard work he did for the good of the cause!

At the Dice'n Cards Saloon and Gambling Emporium, he made his survey again. This time he skipped the beer. There were plenty of places at the gambling tables, but he slid past them. None of the cardsharks looked familiar. There were probably ten wanted men in both the saloons he had been through, but he couldn't keep up on all the wanted posters.

Spur decided he could do no good here and pushed open the saloon swinging doors and walked out on the street. The sun was a half hour from down. The air cooler now, with a touch of the light fragrance of peach blossoms. He hadn't seen a peach tree.

He walked toward the hotel.

"Spur McCoy!" It was an accusation that bellowed into the quiet street from behind him.

Spur stopped, kept his hands well away from his .45. Slowly he turned and saw the only man who could have called him. The man was dressed fancy like a gambler, black hat, sparkling vest and ruffled shirt front under a ribbon thin black string tie. He held a long, thin cigar in his teeth and a snarl on his face. He was short, maybe five-six.

"I figured it was you, no matter what name you're going by. Hear you're a fast draw."

"You heard wrong, stranger. I've never met you before."

"Not good enough, McCoy. Try Joplin, about two years ago. You were a lawman of some kind. You didn't take kindly to a little printing operation I had going."

"I never forget an outlaw's face, and I've never

met yours at Joplin or any other town."

"My good fortune. In Joplin I was the one who got away, clean, with more than twenty thousand in pretty good ten dollar bills."

"The Barnhart Plates. Yes, I remember. At least we got the counterfeiting plates and everyone but you."

"And the twenty thousand. You should know that I passed all but about a thousand of it. Most of it in high stakes poker games. Amazing how many phony bills you can slip through a game."

The short man in the gambler's clothes flexed his right hand where it hung next to a polished six-gun in a well worn holster.

"You remember what happened to Josh?"

"Yes. We told him to drop his weapon. He made a grandstand play and lost."

"Lost his life, but it was enough to let me get away. Promised myself, McCoy, that I was gonna kill you. Never have liked lawmen much."

"You use a .45 caliber derringer, right?"

"Hell, no. Sometimes I carry a derringer, but always a .22, smaller, scares as well as a .45 size and can be effective at close range. Never a .45 derringer. That's my serious weapon size. We've talked enough. Time for you to die. I always like to let my victims know why they're getting shot to death. Only seems right."

"As long as you win. You ever lost, Barnhart?"

"Only in Joplin when my gun hand got hit. But it's healed and well and faster than it was then."

The two men stood on the boardwalk in Dodge City. People coming out of stores and saloons stopped and listened, then backed off and got out of the line of fire. They had seen it happen many times before. Two men with old grudges meet in Dodge and settle the score.

Spur judged the distance as about forty yards. It was much farther than most gunsharps liked. Fifteen yards was the favorite, and ten yards better. Twenty the maximum and even then the six-gun's accuracy dropped off alarmingly.

"McCoy, I don't want this to string out any longer. Two years is plenty. Why don't we make it a Texas walk down?"

Spur heard and remembered two other walk down shootouts he had been in. They were no fun. Each man had one round in his six-gun. On a given signal each was free to walk forward and fire whenever he wanted to. If the first round missed, or only wounded the other man, the one who had not fired could then "walk down" the other man and shoot him from any range he wanted to, even point blank.

The Texas walk down meant that it was certain that one of the two men would die within the next two or three minutes.

"I don't like that kind of fool's game," Spur said evenly. "It's an excuse for a poor marksman. You really that bad with a six-gun that you need a walk down?"

"Hell no, but I want to be certain. Then you won't shoot me in the back the way you did my brother." Barnhart shouted the accusation. Half the town heard him. It was the worst kind of insult to a gunman, especially a lawman.

Spur nodded. "You got what you want, Barnhart.

This is the last day you'll pass counterfeit money." He looked over the growing crowd, picked out a deputy sheriff and waved him forward.

"Deputy Carson here will referee. He'll check the weapons for rounds," Spur called.

Barnhart bobbed his head in agreement.

The deputy, who Spur had talked to from time to time, came up and took Spur's gun. He held it up and punched out four rounds and let them fall in the dirt. He called another man from the crowd who came over and looked in the cylinder.

"Only one round left," the farmer said.

Spur took back the weapon and eased it into leather. This would not be a fast draw contest, not from forty yards, but the ten-inch barrel would be a factor. It meant he had a thirty percent better accuracy at this range than Barnhart did. But what if he missed? The forty yards would be gone in thirty seconds as Barnhard walked down the line and killed Spur McCoy.

Deputy Carson and the sodbuster walked to Barnhart and took his gun. Spur saw it was a standard .45, maybe a Peacemaker. Spur watched the four cartridges drop into the dust. Little boys would be scrambling for the souvenirs in a few minutes even before the blood stopped flowing.

"One round left," the farmer called. The deputy double checked, gave the weapon back to Barnhart butt first and watched him slide it into leather.

The men still stood forty yards apart. Barnhart didn't seem to be worried about the distance. He probably figured both of them would start walking toward each other.

Deputy Carson reached the sidewalk and looked at the two men standing in the middle of the dusty Dodge City street. The whole town seemed to have come to a standstill. More and more people crowded the boardwalks on both sides. Down the street drivers quickly pulled horses up close to the boardwalk to get out of the line of fire.

The deputy looked at both men who indicated they were ready.

"Begin!" Deputy Carson shouted.

Spur turned sideways, as in a formal duel of days gone by, to present a narrower side profile as a target. His right foot went out ahead toward his target but placed at a .45 degree angle and he used a two handed grip on the big .45 after he drew it from leather.

Barnhart had taken one step as he drew his weapon. He stopped and looked at Spur.

"You're bluffing, McCoy. Nobody would risk a shot at this distance. Not in a Texas walk down."

He took another step and stopped.

Spur blinked, sighted in over the groove and blade, then looked at Barnhart. He was standing stock still, facing forward. Now was the time, before he presented a moving target, before he could turn to the side.

Spur realized his life was on the line. This wasn't the usual gun fighting kind of call out. Then, if both men missed, it would be settled for the moment. But now, if either man fired first and missed, the first shooter was a dead man.

McCoy thought of his life so far. It had been full, he had done most of what he wanted to do. It had been a fine, exciting life. Today, as his Indian friends used to say, today was a good day to die.

He sighted in again on the fancy ruffled shirt and slightly to the left of center. Sweat threatened to roll into his right eye. He wiped it away.

"Having second thoughts about such a long try?" Barnhart chided. "Go ahead, waste your shot. Make it easy for me."

Spur took a deep breath, held it, sighted in again. His hands held the big gun rock solid, square on the target. Don't pull, not now, squeeze the trigger. Never know exactly when it's going off. Smooth, stroke it, squeeze, squeeze, squeeze . . . .

It was a surprise when the Colt, long barreled .45 went off. He let the recoil bring his hands upward and to the left as he watched Barnhart.

A thousand thoughts raced through his brain in the fraction of a second it took for the flight of the spinning .45 slug. Had he figured wind? Was there wind? He prayed the powder charge in that particular round had been well packed, was up to strength and was good powder. What if Barnhart moved at the last second? Was his aim true?

The gasp of the crowd came briefly through his mind. Most of them didn't think that he would fire at that range, figured he was bluffing, as did Barnhart.

There was a roar from the crowd of as many as two hundred people when the bullet struck Barnhart. Spur watched in a kind of detached interest as Barnhard staggered to the rear from the impact of the big bullet, then fell on his back in the dust.

"Hold your position, Mr. McCoy!" Deputy

Carson bellowed. Barnhard had dropped his weapon. He lay still for a moment. Someone ran toward him. He moved, rolled to his hands and knees and crawled to the weapon, then slowly, with extreme pain and care, he lifted to his feet.

Barnhard held his left hand over his chest where a growing red stain turned his shirt bright red.

He took two steps, wiped his left hand over his eyes to clear them.

The crowd gasped as his hand left a bloody streak across his forehead and his cheeks.

He took another step forward, lifted the six-gun to waist height, and managed another step. He was still thirty-eight yards away. He had only little more than made up for the distance he had been knocked backward by the heavy .45.

One more step came and the crowd rippled with talk about the man and the shootout. The heavy weapon dragged Barnhart's right hand down and he used both hands to lift the .45. Slowly, ever so slowly, he raised it to eye level and tried to aim.

Spur McCoy stood where he had been a second after he fired, the six-gun still aimed forward, his feet exactly where they had been. Sweat ran into his eyes. His arm ached from the weight of the big gun. Slowly he lowered his arms to his side, slid the weapon in his holster. It could do him no more good.

Now, Barnhart could walk up thirty more yards, put the Peacemaker against Spur's chest and blow his heart into pieces.

Thirty-five yards away, Barnhart shook his head and blinked rapidly, but couldn't seem to clear his eyes.

Barnhart bellowed in rage and tried to run forward. He took two steps, then fell forward in the dust and horse droppings. Furiously he brushed the dry manure aside, struggled to his hands and knees, then teetered as he pushed up to his feet.

Once more he tried to lift the gun. It took both hands. One woman on the boardwalk began to cry.

"My God! Look at him! How can he even move!" A hushed voice asked. In the ear-humming stillness the words flowed across the broad street.

Barnhart took one more step, lifted the weapon with both hands to his waist, and gave a soft cry of anger and fear. He struggled to lift the weapon higher, then he screamed, dropped the .45 and clutched at his chest as he crumpled to the dirt.

Doc Crenshaw ran from the boardwalk in front of the hardware and knelt over Barnhart.

Spur watched with only half his attention. He had thought his round had only scratched Barnhart. Closely, so closely he had almost given himself up for dead. Now with the other man down, Spur tried to relax. Slowly, he realized that this was not his day to die. He gave a shuddering little sigh, and worked out five rounds from his gunbelt and pushed them into the cylinder of his .45. Now was no time to get caught with an empty gun. He took another breath and watched the doctor.

The medic tried for a pulse, then listened to Barnhart's chest. He ripped open the ruffled shirt and saw where the bullet hit home, directly under the heart. It had sliced in half one of the main arteries leading from his heart. The doctor shook his head.

"He's dead," Doc Crenshaw said. He pointed to two men to carry the Barnhart to the undertaker.

Deputy Carson walked over to Spur, a small frown fighting with a grin. "You'll have to write out a report down at the office, Mr. McCoy, or Mr. Smith, whatever." He shook his head. "That shot was over forty yards! Dead center."

Spur felt nothing. He heard the deputy. "Lucky shot," he said.

The deputy laughed softly. "Not a chance. A man doesn't risk that kind of shot if he isn't dead sure he can make it. If you had missed, you'd be on your way now to the undertaker instead of the other guy. Barnhart you called him?"

"I tried to talk him out of it."

"I heard. Let's get the paperwork done. It's time for supper."

For the first time in a month, the thought of food made Spur feel like throwing up.

It took him ten minutes in the sheriff's office to write out a statement and sign it. Deputy Carson signed it as well.

Sheriff Johnson had been making some rounds while it was still daylight and had walked up on the gunfight just before the shot was fired.

"Glad you're on my side, McCoy. I know that's your real name and everybody in town knows about it now. I'd never have the nerve to do that. Never agree to a walk down in the first place. You know I hear folks down in Texas say that's really the Arizona walk down."

Spur mumbled something, got out of there and walked directly back to his room in the hotel. It looked down on the spot of the shootout.

When he caught the doorknob he saw that the panel was unlocked. He drew the .45 and pushed the door open slowly. Lila sat on the bed waiting for him. She was fully dressed and had a book in her hand. She gave a little cry of joy and rushed to him. He closed the door and held her. She had been crying. She lifted her tear stained face to his.

"I was so afraid you were going to be killed down there! I saw the whole thing."

He stroked her hair and led her back to the bed.

"Okay, it's over now, Lila. It's all over. No need for any more tears."

"You could have been killed!"

"Could have. Wasn't."

He was calm now, the reaction of the sudden emotional meeting with Barnhart over. Soon he would have to telegraph Washington that the last of the Barnhart gang was dead and the case should be closed. The twenty thousand in bogus tens was in circulation.

He got Lila's tears stopped and kissed her cheeks and then her nose and at last her lips. She smiled and blew her nose.

"Don't ever scare me that way again, please."

"I'll try. But, like this time, the option is never mine." He watched her and then walked to the window. The street was empty now, with darkness sneaking into the daylight.

"I didn't hear all of it. But your real name is Spur McCoy? Why did you lie to me?"

"I'm doing a job where some people would recognize my name. So I use a different one." He picked up her hand. "I'd bet a dollar your real name isn't Lila Pemberthy."

She looked at him quickly, a frown growing. "Why . . . why do you say that?"

"You're a performer. I knew a singer in Washington who changed her name twice a year so she could get more jobs."

"That's no way to build up a reputation, to keep demanding more money each time."

"This singer wasn't good enough to have a reputation." They both laughed and Spur felt a little better.

"Lila, I'm not in the mood for any supper tonight. You go down without me. I need to sit here and figure out things a little. Do you understand? I always hate it when I have to kill a man, and when I do I have a little bit of rationalization to do, some thinking to get figured out.

"I have to get things right again. Especially when the dead man is one like Barnhart. He wasn't a vicious man, a mad dog killer or a real outlaw. He was just a counterfeiter. Can you understand what I'm saying?"

She bobbed her head and kissed him. "I do. Taking a man's life must be hard on you. At least I'll never have to worry about that." She hesitated. "Oh, should I call you Spur McCoy now, if that's really your name?"

"Might as well, everyone else will."

She laughed softly and touched his crotch.

"Maybe later on you'll show me your spur, the way we had planned this afternoon?"

"I'm not sure. Maybe we should put off the fun and games until tomorrow."

"I understand."

She frowned again and he liked what it did to her pretty face. "Oh, are you still in land speculation?"

"I'm afraid so. A job to do. That's why people might know my name. If they do, they raise the price knowing I have to buy no matter the cost, if my employers tell me to."

"Oh." She sounded disappointed. "I'll stop by after supper before I go to sing at eight." She hugged him and went to the door. "Spur McCoy, you take care of yourself," she said, then grinned and went into the hall, closing his door firmly behind her.

14

McCoy dropped on the bed and lay with his fingers laced behind his head. There had been no way out of the shoot, he knew that, but when an old case came up to haunt him that way, he wondered how soon it would be that some angry man would storm up to him and gun him down without warning. It had happened before to other agents, to other lawmen.

He lay there half an hour thinking about his work with the agency. At last he kicked off the bed, checked his weapon, and filled the empty spaces in his cartridge loops on his belt. It was dark outside, time for him to be moving.

Maybe tonight would be the time he would catch the lawman killer.

It seemed that half of the town knew him now. It was impossible to slip into a saloon unnoticed now and look around. He spent an hour touring the twelve saloons. The barkeeps at most of the spots had seen him before and nodded. By now everyone in town knew that he was a lawman "of some kind" as Barnhart had screamed in the middle of the street.

Those few words had made his job that much harder. He studied every face in each saloon, but there was no twinge of recognition, no face that he hadn't seen once or twice before here in town, or that was new to him. None of the faces could be pegged in Greensburg or the death towns back the stage line toward Wichita.

On his second round of the saloons, Spur sat in on poker games. He had a five dollar limit at each table. If he lost or won five dollars at the quarter limit table, he bowed out and moved on.

It was not good poker on his part as he tried to watch the people in the saloon at the same time. The first place he lost his five dollars and walked across the street to the next saloon. He realized that he hadn't heard Lila sing yet, so he made sure he was at the Silver Dollar Saloon at eight.

He was surprised by the songs she sang. Most of them were sad songs, not the bright bouncy ones she usually used. He caught her eye but she did not come out to his table after she sang. She was down about something, and he decided it would be better to let her work it out.

On his way to the next saloon, the Dangerous Dog, he met Deputy Carson. They talked a minute.

"Today's gonna be one I won't ever forget," Carson said. "Damn, you stood out there forty damn yards and blasted that son-of-a-bitch right in the chest with one shot!"

Spur didn't want to talk about it. He nodded, but he young deputy pressed him.

"That ten-inch barrel, it hard to find a weapon like

that?'' the deputy asked.

"Most any good gunsmith can put one on most any good weapon like a Colt, a Remington, or a Ruger .44 Old Army. You want one ready made get the Wyatt Earp Dixie. It's a .44 with a twelve inch octagon barrel.'' He paused. "Don't count on drawing the Wyatt Earp Dixie in a rush, though, the things hangs half way down your leg."

Deputy Carson laughed. "Won't count on it. Sure would be nice to have more range than twenty yards and hit something. Maybe I'll just cut down a small rifle to about twelve inches and carry that.''

He held out his hand. "Mr. McCoy, sure as hell want to say I learned a lot from you today. Hope to be a better lawman because of it. Hell, I'll be telling my grandchildren about today so often they'll get tired of the story.''

They shook hands.

"Well, I got to move. I'm off at nine-thirty. Then I got a special meeting. Not sure what it's all about, but it does sound interesting. Doubt if it has anything to do with the law though.'' Deputy Carson chuckled. "Hell, you never can tell these days. Thanks again for today.'' He touched his hat brim with his first finger and ambled on down the boardwalk checking each merchant's door as he went.

At the next saloon, Spur paid attention to his poker and was soon seven dollars ahead. He stood, put two dollars in the center of the table.

"Men, I got to leave, but I'll sweeten the next pot for those of you lucky enough to be staying in the game.'' Most of the men around the table smiled.

The biggest loser kept his frown in place but didn't comment.

At nine-thirty Spur noticed the time by his pocket watch. He was deep in the middle of a poker game at the Lonesome Garter Saloon and was two dollars down. He hoped the deputy had a good meeting whatever it was. Spur went back to his cards, but swept the room now and then. He saw no one he figured could be the lawman killer.

Deputy Vic Carson had a bounce to his step as he walked out past the last house on Main Street and waited by the elm tree the way they had agreed. Nothing like this had ever happened to him before. He wasn't exactly sure why it was happening now, but the invitation had been rather explicit.

Five minutes after he got off work they would meet at the elm tree. It was supposed to be secret so he had told nobody. He didn't even want to think about it. But there was the hint that there could be some information about the lawman killer.

If he could help find the gunman who had been cutting down lawmen in Kansas, he would be a hero. He might even get a raise, maybe be a sheriff in his own right somewhere.

He was dreaming dreams so grand that he barely heard the buggy coming down the street. Yes, it was supposed to be a black buggy with the front closed in. He waited. The horse stopped beside him and he opened the side curtain.

"I'm Deputy Carson, and we were to meet here, right?"

There was a low answer and he stepped inside the rig. Almost at once, a muffled report came from the buggy and Deputy Carson slammed against the back cushion, his eyes wide as he realized he had been shot.

It hurt so bad he couldn't think straight. A quick hand stripped the pistol out of his holster and threw it out the far side of the buggy.

His mind refused to believe it, even as the series of smashing pains ripped through him. His gut! He had been shot in the belly, just like all those other dead lawmen back the line toward Wichita! He had read the warnings. He had to tell somebody. He knew who the killer was!

But when he tried to move his legs, they felt like lead sticks. He could barely lift his hands. There was no strength in his arms. His belly burned. He saw the weapon then, a .45 but a derringer! The small little weapon packed a mighty wallop. The gloved hand that held it moved up to his chest directly over his heart.

Billowing pain blocked out his vision. His ears were engulfed with a roaring that wouldn't stop. Somewhere, there was a voice talking, patiently, explaining something, he wasn't sure just what. The voice droned on and on. Sometimes it was clear and words made sense, then his mind became a jumbled mass of visions and sounds and memories and nothing meant anything.

He had to do something or he would be dead soon. Maybe he could lunge at the killer. Smash into the hand holding the gun, grab it and turn it against the maniac.

At once Deputy Carson knew that was impossible. He could barely speak. His words came out jumbled and unreal. How had he gone to pieces so quickly?

What had happened to all of his dreams? He was only twenty-four years old. That was too young to die!

The voice had faded. Only a few of the words he heard made sense. "Have to die," he had heard those words several times. It couldn't be true! This couldn't be happening to him.

Slowly, his eyes focused again and he saw the small gun coming toward him out of the blackness.

"No!" he blurted. The word was firm, solid. "Don't kill me!"

The gun came closer. He tried to swing his wooden arm at it. Nothing moved. He tried to butt it with his head, but his chin only hit his chest.

His eyes widened as the muzzle came closer and closer. Then it touched his chest just over his heart.

He tried to scream, but only a babble of sounds came out. Again the pain boiled through his body, tearing him apart, dimming his vision, blocking his hearing. When his eyes cleared the weapon's muzzle pressed against his chest.

His mind heard the explosion a millisecond before the terrible pain stabbed through his chest, the .45 lead slug plowed through his heart and it was over. He didn't hurt anymore.

Deputy Carson couldn't smell his burning shirt or the charred flesh around the wound from the powder burns. He couldn't see the round black ring, nor could he feel the buggy move slightly as a figure stepped out of it and closed the side curtain.

Then the killer whacked the horse on the rump, sending her trotting down the road, the reins trailing along beside and under the buggy as the startled animal kept going for nearly half a mile before she stopped in the darkness and began nibbling at the few shoots of grass at the side of the trail.

Spur McCoy tired of the poker. He sat at the bar and watched the men in the room, drinking, gambling, and grabbing at the two dance hall girls who circulated around the tables selling drinks and offering anything and everything else for sale upstairs.

Tonight the price was a dollar for a quick one and two dollars for anything you could do in half an hour.

Spur went back to the jail and made sure the sheriff was safely tucked in his cell.

"Do a lot of Dodge City townfolks good to see you in there, Sheriff Johnson," Spur said keeping a straight face.

"So bring them through and charge them a dime a head to take a look," Johnson said. "A couple nights like that and I can retire and move to Denver. Never been there but that's where I'm going when I can. One of my big dreams is to live a mile in the sky. Can you imagine that?"

"It isn't like you can step off the edge of Denver and fall a mile down," Spur said.

"A man can always hope." The sheriff scowled at Spur. "It's too damn quiet around here. How long has it been since Sheriff Bjelland in Greensburg went down?"

"Eight, nine days, not sure. Time seems not to be a factor in these killings."

"Remember, I said I'd stay in here a week and that's it. Then I'm back on the town doing my job. My deputies are holding up well, but they're overworked."

"You make an appointment with the killer and I'll be glad to cut him up into pieces and serve him to you for breakfast," Spur said. "If you're bitching, you're all right. Keep your spirits up and keep that loaded six-gun handy."

"No doubt about that, city slicker. I didn't just get into town with a trail drive from Mexico."

Spur waved and checked with the deputy who came on at nine-thirty. Everything was quiet. Not even a gunfight tonight.

"Things will pick up about midnight," Spur said and ambled over to the Silver Dollar Saloon to catch Lila's eleven o'clock song fest.

She came out smiling and sassy, and Spur saw a much happier and interesting Lila than had sung at eight. All of her songs were upbeat and only one from the Civil War, "The Bloody Mongahela," made it into the show. She closed with "Jimmy Cracker" and "Rosie You are My Posy" and "The Girl I Left Behind." The applause was honest and continuous. She came back and sang one encore that had a touch of sadness: "My Love, My True Love Has Left Me."

Lila had spotted Spur during the last song and winked. After the applause died, she came out to his table and had a cup of coffee that the barkeep always provided her.

"Howdy, tall stranger, you new in these parts?" she asked with a try at a Western twang. She broke up laughing as she finished it.

"Shore am, Little Filly. Anybody got a halter on you yet?" Spur went along with the game. Soon they both were laughing.

"You really worked for a U.S. senator the way you told me? Or was that all gully washing raspberry juice just to confuse a poor lonesome, inexperienced virgin like me?"

"Really. He was an old family friend. Now Washington is a town where you can meet some strange people." He hesitated. "Oh, I bought a new bottle of white wine, want to test it out?"

"Yes. Now."

They walked out of the saloon as several of the men who had just heard her sing, called to thank her. She waved back at them and soon they were on the street heading for their hotel.

She held his arm tightly.

"Are you all right, Lila? You seem a little tense."

"No, no, I'm fine. I always get wound up as I perform. The energy keeps me going and then suddenly it's all over. I need to relax and let everything slow down."

"With some good wine."

"Or anything else you want to give me . . . or put to me."

She started walking faster, looking up at him. "I can almost feel your hands on me now, all over me!"

Spur chuckled. "Not right here on the street or in the lobby. Try to control yourself for a few more minutes."

"I'll try."

She held his arm as they went up the front steps. "What's this talk I hear about people saying that you're a law officer of some kind? Is that true?"

"I came here to buy land. If the people think I'm some kind of marshal or something, that will be a help to me."

"But they said the man who was killed was a counterfeiter, and he accused you of killing his brother and you said you got the engraving plates. You must have been a lawman."

They went up the steps toward the third floor.

"Yes, I was a law officer for a while, in Joplin. We helped some men from Washington get the plates back. That was it. I quit the job and moved to Chicago. I never expected this Barnhart ever to see me again."

She watched him a moment as he turned her key in the lock and swung open the door.

"All right, Spur McCoy. I can believe that. It sounds right, and I want to believe it." Her sober mood changed. She touched his crotch, then leaned up and kissed him. "Now, where is wine and where is that big sexy stick of yours?"

He held up his hand. "The wine is down in my room, I'll be right back."

She already had her dress unbuttoned down the front. These buttons went all the way to the hem of the dress, over fifty of them.

"I'll let you go if you swear on a stack of land deeds that you'll be right back."

"I so swear." He reached down and pushed his face past the dress buttons and kissed the very top of her bare breasts.

"Get out of here and hurry back!" she yelped.

Spur made it in record time. She sat on the bed,

naked, waiting for him when he opened the door.

"What took you so long?" she asked.

He worked the cork out of the bottle with a puller and poured the pale white wine in the two glasses she had set on the dresser. She sipped it, and nodded, then drained half the glass.

"Good," she said. "Now me."

Spur shook his head silently as he stared at her young, delightful, unmarked body. A woman was all curves and grace and perfect line and motion. Especially her breasts.

"Remember, I said this couldn't be an all night affair. I still have some thinking through things to do."

"Just once, then quickly before I explode. You don't even have to undress, kind of like you were forcing me to fuck you."

"It's not as good that way," he said.

"Sometimes it's better for me. Just this once, be rough with me . . . a little rough."

Before she finished talking he pushed her down on the bed, held her arms spread at the side over her head and rammed her legs widely apart. With one hand he opened his pants and wedged out his erection. With no preliminaries at all he bent and rammed at her.

He felt the dry skin burning, eased off, let her juices flow a little and then drove into her with one quick thrust that brought a cry of pain and delight from her that was all mixed up. He held her hands spread wide as he powered at her, feeling his pelvic bones grinding against hers, then coming out almost all the way and ramming back so hard he pushed her two inches up the bed with every thrust.

"Yes, yes!" she crooned.

Ten more powerful plunges and he was on fire. He didn't know if he could perform again that day or not. He exploded with a raging fury that he knew was part of his anger for the death in the afternoon, yet part was pure animal passion. He held the final thrust until every drop of fluid had jetted out of him and then he came away from her and buttoned his pants.

"You wanted fast and hard. Was that fast enough for you?" He bent and kissed her cheek. She rolled toward him. He slapped her soft botton twice and walked to the door.

"Enjoy the wine," he said and slipped into the hall. He had a few more pegs to put in the right holes before he could get to sleep that night.

There had been too many interruptions on this case, too many side problems to clear up. He had to pick out the killer damn soon, or the whole thing would dissolve into chaos and the lawman killer would probably fade into the landscape and never be found. Tomorrow. Tomorrow had to be the day.

15

Spur heard about Deputy Carson at breakfast. He left the rest of his food and ran directly to the sheriff's office.

Sheriff Johnson sat behind his desk. They had not moved the body. The buggy had not been missed until morning and when it was found, the owner came straight to the sheriff.

"What the hell is going on here? Has this crazy maniac started killing any lawman he can find?" Sheriff Johnson shuddered and wiped wetness away from his eyes.

"That boy was like a son to me. I brought him into this business, taught him everything I know. He was good. Smart, ambitious . . . damn!"

"Let's go out to the scene," Spur said gently. "There might be something we can find this time."

They rode out to the buggy. The reins had been tied by the owner before he came back. He sat along side the road waiting for them. He held a six-gun.

The man's name was Billy Earlly. He handed the weapon to the sheriff as soon as they dismounted.

"Found this back by the elm tree there just at the edge of town. Looks like the rig stopped there for a while. There's some droppings there and some footprints, but I couldn't make out much of it."

"Thanks, Bill," Sheriff Johnson said. "That's Carson's sidearm. He was proud of that piece. Sent to Chicago for it."

They walked over to the buggy. Both front curtains were closed. Deputy Carson lay sprawled in the rig. The smell of charred cloth clung in the air. Spur reached in and checked his chest, and his belly.

"Two shots, just like before, Sheriff. I'd say it's the same killer. Same method, even down to the stolen buggy." Spur looked over the body, the pockets, then the rest of the inside of the buggy. He could not find anything that would help. Nothing had been dropped or left. There was no sign who had sat in the other seat when Deputy Carson was killed.

The sheriff looked it all over as well. At last they had Bill Earlly lead the horse and rig back to the undertaker.

The two men rode back to the spot where the owner said he found the pistol.

Spur stopped ten yards away, let the reins down on his mount and walked up to the buggy tracks in the road dirt. The tracks were plain enough, and the droppings told where the horse had stood for at least a short time.

Footprints? He went over the dusty part again. There were prints on the right side of the rig, but on the other side the ground was harder, blown bare by the wind. He could make out only a few plain men's boot tracks on the far side. Nothing distinctive about them. They probably matched Carson's boots and a hundred others in town.

"The killer took Carson's gun away here and threw it out. He might even have killed Carson here, then chased the horse down the trail."

"Which left only a short walk back through town," Spur said. There was nothing more for them to do there. On the way back to the office they checked the undertaker. He confirmed that death was due to gunshot, probably a large caliber, .44 or .45 at muzzle-touching range.

A few minutes later behind his desk in his office, Sheriff Johnson sighed. "One deputy dead, another one shot up. I'm down to two deputies. Means I got to work the street tonight."

"Not a chance!" Spur said sharply. "The killer went for a deputy because you were safe and secure. He'd just trying to lure you out of your protection. Stay put one more night."

"Hell, I guess it's better than dead." He stood and paced around his office. "Christ! I feel so helpless. What the hell am I supposed to do, McCoy?"

"If I knew, I'd be doing it myself. I'm as frustrated as you are. No clues, no suspects, just bodies turning up. God damn! I'm going for a ride, try to blow some of the fuzzy thinking out of my brain." He stopped on his way to the door. "Frank, today and tonight, you be double damn careful, you hear?"

Frank waved. He was cleaning his pair of .44 six-guns.

Spur rented a horse and rode three miles out in the

prairie. He sat there staring into the endless plains, then turned around and rode hard for a mile toward town, then eased off and walked the bay toward the stable.

He had figured out exactly nothing on the ride, but it made him feel better. He put the horse back in the livery and went to the undertaker to see if he had cut out the bullet. He had found one of them. It was banged up a little, but there was no doubt, it was a .45. Why didn't a big powder charge like that drive the slug right on through his belly and out his back? Especially fired that close? Low powder charge? He'd met the same question before.

All day Spur walked the streets watching the people. He was on hand for the morning stage. The only people who left was one grandma and her teenage grandson, and a salesman heading back toward Wichita. He wasn't interested in the incoming passengers.

If the killer hadn't ridden out of town on his own horse, he was still around. All Spur had to do was find him out of Dodge City's two thousand people, and maybe those on the farms and ranches nearby.

In his whole career, Spur McCoy had never come up against a case like this. Bodies dropping all over the state and he had absolutely nothing solid to work with. Worse, he had no suspects. The killer could be anyone: a teenage boy trying to make a name for himself, an old drunk panhandling himself from town to town, a just out of prison bank robber taking his anger out on all lawmen.

He had dinner with Lila at the hotel that noon. She was bouncy and full of energy.

"Let's go for a ride down the little stream this afternoon in a buggy and have a picnic about four o'clock."

Spur shook his head automatically. "Sorry, I have some work to do."

"Land buying? You don't talk much about it."

"That's the way it is with secret negotiations."

Somehow, he didn't think that she believed his land scheme cover story any more. It didn't matter that much. He had a much larger problem.

That afternoon he checked the three stores that sold guns. No, there had been no unusual sale of a weapon to anyone. Just a couple of cowboys, a drummer who wanted a small derringer in a .22 caliber for protection, and a farmer getting a new shotgun to use on pheasants.

He stopped in the middle of the street as he was crossing to the next gunsmith. Why had he decided to stay here? Why not move on down the stage line. Why was Dodge different? Slowly it came to him.

In every other town, the killer had cut down the top lawman. Here it had been only a deputy. He was starting to think like the killer. The man wanted the sheriff, but he'd take a deputy, waiting his chance on Sheriff Johnson.

Made sense. Spur was counting on being right about that. He continued his rounds. He was going to be evident, out on the streets, walking, watching, checking parked buggies on Main Street or anywhere else he saw them where they seemed to be out of place. Spur was determined to walk Dodge City until dawn!

Lila Pemberthy sang beautifully at eight. She was in fine voice, and enjoyed her work. She thanked the barman for the cup of coffee and slipped out the back door of the Silver Dollar Saloon and walked quickly toward a small building she had selected that afternoon.

It was time. She had thought it through and knew it would work. She still wore her performing dress and carried a fancy reticule. There was time, lots of time.

She slipped on a hat that fit closely around her hair and sat low over her eyes, then edged out to the street from the alley. No one was in sight. She left the alley, turned down the street and walked two blocks.

She saw no one. Half a block ahead was the vacant four room house she had selected. She walked to it, looked up and down the dark street and saw no one, so moved confidently to the back of the structure and the small open porch. There she took out a quart of coal oil she had stolen from the saloon. They kept it for their dozens of lamps.

She tried the back door. It was open. Quickly she moved inside to the bedroom. There were still curtains up, and some furniture, including a bed and blankets. Without wasting any motions, she assembled some papers, a sheet from the bed, and a wooden chair. She set them against a wall and poured the coil oil over the whole thing, saturating the wall. Then from her reticule she took some matches and lit the stack on fire. It burned up well. There was only a tiny window in the room so no one would see the flames for some time.

Lila went out the back door, through the vacant lot behind the house and around to another street. She walked back to Main and waited in the shadows. No one saw her. Lila could be patient when she had to be, and this was one of those times.

It was nearly half an hour before she heard someone yell "Fire!" It was another five minutes before someone ran into the sheriff's office and reported the fire. The volunteer fire brigade assembled at the now furiously burning house, but there was little they could do.

As soon as the report came, the deputy sheriff rushed out of the office and ran down the street.

Lila moved quickly to the sheriff's office door and slipped inside. She looked around, then went straight to the desk and found the keys to the cells. She took the right one and put it in her reticule. Then she opened the door to the cell room.

Sheriff Johnson lay snoring softly on the double mattress in the first cell. The door was not even locked. Lila closed the door into the outer part of the office and threw a bolt. Then she moved in beside the sheriff and saw the pistols at his side.

Carefully she lifted them and slid them far under the bunk where he could not reach them. She put on thin black gloves, then took from her purse a derringer and pressed it against Sheriff Johnson's slightly paunchy belly.

She slapped his face firmly.

"What? What . . ." His eyes focused and he blinked. "The singer, Lila. What you doing here?"

She shot him. The bullet crashed into his belly tearing up essential organs and plowing upward, doing more damage than she had really intended.

Sheriff Johnson passed out.

She slapped him back to consciousness. He roused slowly, the pain coursing through his body evident on his face.

"Christ, you gut shot me! Damned derringer. Damned woman! You're the one who killed Carson, and the rest!"

"Sheriff, I don't know what you're talking about. You killed my Robert, and I swore an oath to myself that I would repay you. I told myself that someday I'd come back to this Kansas town and I'd kill you. To even the scales of justice because you killed my Robert."

"Lila, I never met you before last week when you come to town to sing!" He said it over the grinding, wrenching pain that gushed into his brain and set his whole torso on fire.

"Liar! You are all liars! If I must I'll remind you what happened. Been several years ago now, six or seven, I lose track. Robert and me just come in from Texas in our little wagon ahunting a place to farm. You folks in Kansas didn't treat us right good.

"You kept hitting Robert and knocking him down. I didn't know why. I said: Why you doing that, Sheriff? He ain't hurtin' you. I was little more than a girl then, just seventeen, and married only two months with a Texas sunbonnet hiding most of my long brown hair. I wore a cheap calico dress that covered me from wrists to neck to shoe soles. I was only five feet tall but I could get right mad.

"Then you slammed your revolver down across Robert's face, driving him to his knees. Blood gushed from scrapes on his forehead and check and when Robert tried to talk, his jaw didn't work right.

" 'Stop it, stop it!' I shouted.

"You said: 'Shut up, you little poon. I'll take care of you later.' You was a big one, over six feet, with a week's growth of beard and a shiny sheriff's star pinned to your shirt pocket.

"You glared at Robert and told us nobody sassed the sheriff there in Willow. You said you had laws about that sort of thing. You called Robert a scrawny little snot and said lots of unkind things about him. Told him he'd know better next time. 'We call it teaching Texas no-counts to be proper,' is the way you said it that day.

"I screamed at you that he didn't hurt you none. But I moved away a little as I said it, cause you scared me something terrible. You just glared at Robert on the ground.

"You yelled at Robert. 'You gonna hold your tongue now you damn Texas Rebel?'

"Poor Robert got to his knees, then struggled to stand. He was weaving, working hard just to stand up. But he stared hard at you, Sheriff.

"He said: 'Suh, ah don't apologize to white trash like you!'

"Then you went crazy. Your big fist lashed out, hit poor Robert's chin and snapped his head back. He fell in the dirt in front of the hardware store. You bellowed something about him being a rebel. 'My kid brother got shot to death by bastards just like you in the war.' Then you kicked Robert in the side with your heavy boot. Robert curled in a ball.

"You dragged him to his feet, held his shirt front

and pounded your fist into Robert's face again and again. Robert's nose spurted blood. You laughed. You closed one of his eyes and tore his ear. Robert's head flopped from side to side each time you hit him.

"I kept yelling at you to stop. Yelling for somebody to help us. But nobody came. A man and a woman on the boardwalk hurried past. A cowboy walking his horse down the street went to the far side and rode on quickly.

" 'Why won't somebody help us?' I screamed.

"Then you slammed a hard punch into Robert's jaw and he slumped to the ground. You glared at me and yelled. 'Woman, you shut your mouth or I'm gonna pitch you right in jail!'

"Then you kicked Robert again. You called him an ugly little Texas Rebel bastard. 'I'll teach you damn Rebs not to come into my town and insult anybody!' You kicked him hard in the stomach, then aimed for his crotch but missed, so you slammed your boot into Robert's head. When Robert brought his hands up to protect his head, you kicked him in the side again, breaking a rib.

" "Stop it! Stop it! Stop it!' I screamed. 'Won't somebody help Robert?' I watched five or six people on the boardwalk who could hear me. They turned away. So I jumped up and I raced at you, my hands clawing at your face. Before you got your arms up, my right hand finger nails scratched down your cheek leaving three deep marks that filled with blood.

"You bellowed at me, grabbed me and threw me into the dirt. 'Your turn is coming, you southern cunt! You're next, just as soon as I finish with this little bastard!' You turned back to Robert and kicked him again where he lay in the dust. You kicked him twice more in the head.

"All I could do was sob where I lay in the street. I had fallen on fresh horse droppings, but I didn't have the strength to move away from them.

"Remember? You felt your cheek and swore at me. You said we made a good pair, a rebel and his bitch. You told us to get out of town before dark, that you didn't want Texas rabble in your town. Then you spit on Robert and walked into a saloon.

"I crawled over to Robert, saw the ugly bruises on his face and head. So I cradled his head in my lap. I figured he'd come around in a few minutes, and we'd get into the wagon and drive out of your terrible town.

"I sat there for half an hour and Robert didn't move. Wagons went around us in the street. People passing on the boardwalk slowed and looked, but nobody came to help us.

"I told Robert he'd feel better soon, and we'd move on to a friendly little town where we could start farming.

"Then pretty soon a man knelt down beside us. He had a black bag and said he was Doc Smathers. He touched Robert and pinched his nose, then felt of his wrist, and at last put his ear down on Robert's chest.

"I asked the doctor if Robert was hurt bad and he nodded. Said he was hurt as bad as a body can be. He said he was sorry, but that . . . that . . . that Robert was dead! I screamed and wailed and fell on Robert and wouldn't let the doctor touch him again.

I screeched that the doctor was wrong. But somehow I knew he must be right.

"I told him the sheriff killed him, kicked him in the head. But the doctor said that was just the way things were. Said it would get better. But you, as sheriff, was running things. Said your term ended a year ago, but you wouldn't let anybody run for office. Nobody in town would stand up to you."

Lila sighed. She shook her head and frowned at the lawman who had killed her Robert. She was positive this was the man. Lila waved the little gun at Sheriff Johnson who shook his head.

"That ain't me you're talking about. I never met you before last week. You're all confused about it, Lila. Run and get Doc for me and we'll all be friends here. We love you here in Dodge City."

It was a long speech for him. Sheriff Johnson sagged against the mattress. He didn't know where his strength went. He could hardly move his hand. He should be slapping away that funny little derringer and locking her up for the murder of six lawmen. Or was it seven or eight now? He wanted to close his eyes. He was tired. Damn, but it hurt!

"You're trying to trick me. I've seen others try it. Deny that they even knew me. I saw you kick my husband to death! You can't deny anything. Right now we even up the score. I might be from Texas, but I can pull a trigger good as any stinking damn Yankee!"

She put the muzzle of the derringer against Sheriff Johnson's chest, over his heart, and pulled the trigger. The second round from the derringer blasted through shirt and ribs and tore into his heart, killing him instantly.

192

Lila hummed softly as she put the derringer in her reticule, closed it and walked calmly to the back of the jail and opened the bolt on the back door. She looked out cautiously, then walked into the alley and back to the rear door of the Silver Dollar Saloon.

She went in and slipped in to the small room the owner let her use while she sang there. It held a cot where she could rest between her performances.

She put her reticule under the cot and lay down. A soft smile crept over her face. She would have no trouble sleeping now.

"Good night, dearest Robert," she said softly.

That night at eleven, Lila Pemberthy gave the best performance of her career. She sang two encores and told the cheering group that she could stay only two more days in Dodge, then she had to return to St. Louis for an engagement in the opera house. She invited all of them to come see her the next two nights.

Lila left the saloon looking everywhere, but she could not find that nice Mr. Spur McCoy. She wondered what he was up to tonight.

16

Spur had rushed to the site of the fire as soon as he
saw the flames and heard the fire bell which boomed
out three times. He had soon learned in the West
that it was the duty of every able bodied man to
assist in a fire call.

Often it was only a bucket brigade but every man
helped. Spur got there in time to see the roof cave in.
It had been a small one story house, but the fire
must have burned half of it out before anyone saw
the flames break through to the outside.

By that time all they could do was wet down the
shingle roof of a house fifty feet away, and watch
down wind for any sparks that might catch something else on fire.

Spur found out that no one had been living in the
house. The woman who lived closest said she
thought she had seen a figure come out of the place a
half hour before she saw the fire, but she couldn't be
sure.

If no one lived there, how could a fire start? Soon
the theory surfaced that a drifter must have been

there, maybe started a fire by a lighted cigarette. No one had seen smoke coming from the chimney.

The head of the Dodge City Volunteer Firemen was Ivan Lane, who ran the hardware. He had the situation well in hand. He used a short bucket brigade of twenty men to pass buckets of water from the closest pump and had managed to wet down the outside walls and pushed one into the fire after it weakened.

Spur left it up to him and walked back toward the sheriff's office with a deputy and Galloway.

"Somebody told me about the fire and I rushed right down here," Deputy Galloway said. "We don't have a fire too often. I guess it's sort of a social affair. My dad used to say you saw friends you never saw anywhere else except at a fire or a funeral."

"Who else is on duty tonight with you?" Spur asked.

"Who else? Just me and the sheriff sleeping in the jail. Hell, we're down to two deputies now with . . ." Deputy Galloway looked in surprise as Spur began to run. The deputy caught up with him.

"You left the sheriff *alone in the jail!*" Spur growled at him. "Don't you have any sense at all?"

"You mean someone might try to . . . to hurt the sheriff, right there in the jail?"

"Damn right that's what I mean! How long you been gone from the jail?"

"Fifteen, maybe twenty minutes. At the most twenty-five." The deputy had to rush to keep up with Spur.

"How long would it take to fire two .45 rounds?" Spur asked and ran faster as he rounded the corner and sprinted for the front of the sheriff's office and jail six doors down.

Inside the office it all looked normal.

Spur breathed a sigh of relief. Then he tried the door into the jail cells.

"This usually locked?" Spur asked.

"Not when I've been here," Deputy Galloway said. "I think it has a bolt or a bar inside."

"The back door!" Spur bellowed. They both ran out the front and down to the end of the block and raced through the alley to where the jail backed up to the service drive.

The back door was closed. It just might be all right, Spur hoped as he reached for the doorknob. There was no lock on the outside. He turned the knob and pulled the door open. One lamp near the front through a storage room and past the four cells gave off a faint light.

Spur ran to it and turned up the wick. He looked in the first cell where he could see the double mattress the sheriff always used.

"Damnit, no!" Spur bellowed with such hurt and pain that the deputy sheriff rushed forward. Spur bolted into the cell. He saw the sheriff lying on the mattress as if he were asleep. But etched on his body were the familiar powder burns and Spur knew there was no need to check for signs of life. Somebody had murdered the sheriff in his own jail!

"The fire!" Spur bellowed. "The damn fire was a diversion to draw you out of here!" Spur yelled at the deputy. "Whoever it was knew the sheriff was in here, and got rid of you the easy way. Otherwise you'd be dead right now, too."

He opened the bolt on the door into the sheriff's office, went through the door and slumped in a chair. Spur bounced to his feet a minute later.

"You're in charge here now, Galloway. Close that back door to the cells and lock it, then close this one and don't tell anybody about this until morning and I give you the word. I'm a government lawman, with the Secret Service. I'm in town to try to find out who has been killing all the lawmen in Kansas. You've got to help me. Do you understand?"

Galloway sat down in a chair and nodded. "Damn, why did I run out to the fire?"

"It's what you would normally do. It's done now and that we can't change. Help me find out who did it. You just stay here, and don't tell anyone what happened. Do you understand?"

"Yes, sir."

Spur trotted back to the fire. Most of the flames were out. He talked to the head volunteer fire chief, Ivan Lane.

"Notice anything funny about the fire?" Spur asked.

Lane was a square set man, no nonsense, honest as a twenty dollar gold piece. He shook his head.

"Can't right say. Why?"

"I think it was deliberately set. You ever smelled a coal oil set fire?"

"Yep. Smell never does burn out."

"Get your nose warmed up, let's see what we can smell around the edges."

It took them half an hour as the bucket men kept throwing water on the dying fire. Then on the far side, Lane yelled at Spur.

When Spur went around to where Lane was, he had both hands on his hips. "Damn, McCoy, I think we've got something. Not very strong, like maybe less than a gallon, quart maybe. But it's there. Coal oil for damned sure. The smell don't go away."

"Maybe there was a lamp inside," Spur said.

"Not so. Woman next door said a family moved out and took what they could. They showed her through to see if she wanted anything left. She said there wasn't a lamp or a stove or anything like that left to start a fire."

"Show me," Spur said.

They went as close as they could to the still hot skeleton of one wall and sniffed. Spur put his head between the framing and sniffed some more.

"Yes, it's there. You sell coal oil at your store?"

"Of course. Pump it out of a barrel off the back dock. Been doing that for fifteen years."

"You sell any today to someone who might not ordinarily use it?"

Lane thought a minute. "Nope. Sold a gallon to a saloon owner, and another gallon to Mrs. Burdock. Known her for thirty years. She buys a gallon about twice a year for her lamp. She is a thrifty person."

"The barrel is outside your store in back. So someone could pump themselves a gallon or a quart after hours and you'd never know it?"

"Could happen. Don't think it did. I leave the pump in a certain position. It was that way when I used it this morning and when I left tonight."

"Thanks, Mr. Lane. I'm grasping at straws in the tornado here. Don't mention this to anyone else, all right?"

Spur walked rapidly back to the jail.

Deputy Galloway was unravelling like a half knit sweater. He shook and wouldn't look Spur in the eye.

"Galloway, go home. Get out of here and forget what happened and go to sleep. Come in tomorrow when you feel like it. We'll simply close up the jail tonight. When does the other deputy come on board?"

"Eight in the morning."

"Fine. Get out of here."

Galloway looked at the closed door leading to the cells. He shuddered then bolted for the front door. He had forgotten to take his six-gun with him.

Spur let him go. He went in and searched the cell around the body. He spent an hour doing it, going over every inch of the place.

There was nothing there, only a dead body with the usual powder burns on the clothing and flesh. Spur sat on the mattress beside the bed.

"Who?" he said, as if fully expecting the sheriff to answer him. Then he remembered that Frank Johnson said he would try to tell Spur who it was who had killed him if at all possible. He looked over everything again.

Spur studied the body more closely. How could Frank have left a message? By writing something! How could he do that? There was no paper or pencil there. With blood!

Spur checked Frank's clothes in detail. He had seen blood on his shirt. Only a flicker of blood showed on his chest over his heart. Below at his belly there was a much larger red stain.

He had been belly shot first, and bled for several minutes. McCoy checked every inch of Frank's shirt front, then his pants. McCoy's eyes widened. On Frank's right leg he saw what looked like letters. He moved so he could see it from Frank's viewpoint and looked again. There was a strong "L" written in blood, what looked like another letter and then what could be a "B."

They could be the initials of someone's name. L.B. meant nothing to him. L.D. produced little as well. Lane, Ivan Lane was the fire chief. He hardly seemed like a suspect. Spur could think of Larry, Lester, Lewis or Lawrence. He blew out the lamp and closed the door into the cells. He turned out all but one lamp, which he set low in the office, and went out the front door, making sure the night lock clicked into place behind him.

It was too much for him to batter through tonight. What he needed was a good night's sleep and a fresh start in the morning. He had to figure it out right here. There was a good chance that the sheriff knew his killer and he had tried to tell him. The man had dipped his finger in his own belly wound for blood to write down the letters! He must have been positive of the name of the killer.

At the hotel, Spur went up the steps and down to his room where he checked his door silently. Unlocked. He drew his gun, even though he guessed who was inside.

Spur edged the door open and saw the light, turned low, then the brown head of hair on his pillow and the shapely form of his favorite songbird sleeping naked on his bed. He slid into the room, locked the door and slipped out of his pants and shirt. Gently Spur edged over one of Lila's legs so he could lay beside her.

As soon as he stretched out, she rolled over on top of him and kissed his lips. Then leaning up she watched him, her eyes bright.

"So you thought you could sneak in on me and take advantage of me while I was sleeping? No such luck." She kissed him again. "Why didn't you tell me you were with the United States Secret Service and that you were trying to find the man who has been killing all of those lawmen? I found your orders. You are a naughty boy for lying to me."

Spur sat up and turned the wick higher in the lamp. The room filled with light.

"So spank me or something for being naughty," he said. "You were a bad girl yourself."

She frowned, looked at him quickly. "Whatever do you mean by that, Secret Service Agent Spur McCoy?"

"You changed your name, and you don't tell all these Yankees that you're from New Orleans."

The tenseness went out of her face and she relaxed. Lila giggled, then leaned over and kissed him.

"Okay, we're even. I don't care if you're a detective or a lawman or a butcher or saddlemaker. I'm falling in love with you and if you're not careful you're going to wind up getting married. There, I said it."

He held up his hand. "There is always that delicious problem to worry about." He stared at her more serious now. "You know that I hid my orders and my credentials. You had to dig pretty deep in my gear to find them. Why was it so important that you find out for sure what I do?"

She caught one of his hands and used it to cover a breast.

"I was just curious. You seem to be at the sheriff's office a lot. And I've not seen you talking with any local landowners. Then that man said you were a lawmen. I just kind of figured he'd know what he was talking about before he risked his life in a gun fight against you. It made me more curious."

"What if I get mad and throw you out in the hall all bare assed the way you are?"

"I'd start knocking on doors until I found some lonesome man who would take care of me."

Spur had to grin. It was exactly what she would do. He let the frown fall away.

"All right. I'm not angry with you any more, but I've got another problem. Sheriff Johnson was murdered tonight. I have to find out who did it before the guy gets out of town."

"You'll check the stage and the livery stable."

"Already covered. I've got to play detective and do it damn good and damn fast."

"Let me help!"

"No, that could put you in danger. This is my job and I have to do it. Now, you mentioned something about marriage. Let's pretend that we're married."

"Oh, yes, that's what I've been waiting for!"

"Good." Spur snuggled down in the pillow without touching her.

"Hey, we're married, let's see how many times we can make love tonight," she cooed.

"Not tonight, Lila, I told you that I have a hard day at work tomorrow."

She swung a pillow and hit him in the face. He swung one back and for five minutes they had a pillow fight that left them both gasping and laughing and in each other's arms.

The kiss was long and flaming and when it ended he caught her breasts and petted them tenderly.

"But just once. I really do have a lot of work to do tomorrow."

"Whatever you say, lover, whatever you say."

He pushed her on her back and suckled at her mounds. She stroked his hair and found his crotch and petted him.

"Maybe we could make it three times?" she asked.

"Questions, always questions." He rolled over hugging her so she stayed on top and kept licking her breasts.

"Standing up," she said.

"What?"

"Make love to me standing up! I've never been able to. Show me how!"

"This is not a classroom."

"More the pity. Come on, let's fuck standing up!"

She bounced out of bed and grabbed his hand pulling him with her. Spur groaned and followed. He pushed her against the wall.

"Now jump up and put your legs around me and lock them together in back."

"You're joshing me."

"No, not at all, try it."

She did and leaned her back against the wall.

Lila giggled. "This is starting to feel strange."

"It gets better." He loosened her legs a little, holding her bare bottom, then lifted her and bent backwards until his shaft matched her slot and he edged forward.

Lila shrieked in surprise and delight.

"My God! We can do it!"

Spur drove into her until they were firmly locked together pelvic bone to pelvic bone. Her legs were locked behind him and she leaned against the wall with her arms fast around his neck.

"Of course, it helps if one or the other of us has good balance."

She ignored his jibe and leaned close to his ear. "That feels so wonderful! I don't know how you did it, but please do it now, fuck me so hard I'll never forget this time tonight!"

Spur growled at her, kissed her soft lips, then her nose and thrust, came almost out and jammed into her again with such sudden force that she gasped and flattened against the wall.

"Jesus!" she breathed.

Spur made the same slow withdrawal and then the pile driver thrust again and again, gradually increasing the tempo. After five deep penetrations she billowed into a climax that sent her into spasms of unending gasping and moaning and soft little kitten noises deep in her throat.

Her hips got into the act, punching hard against his and rotating as her vaginal muscles gripped him in a shattering series of motions that pushed him almost over the edge. He slowed his stroke and stayed with her, then when she at last tapered off and hugged him so tight he thought he would collapse, he picked up the tempo.

"Yes! Yes! Yes! Yes!" Lila crooned. "Do it again, again. I love it this way. Promise me we can always fuck this way, just forever and forever!"

Then he couldn't respond. He was over the edge, roaring and racing down with an avalanche of power and drive and surging thrusts that jolted his hips harder and harder until he vaporized and the stars and the moon went sliding past him as he shot into the space around them and circled the sun and came back with one final thrust of his hips hard against her.

Slowly he sagged toward the floor. First his knees bent and she slid down a foot. Then another foot and he went down on his knees. She unhooked her legs from behind him and he leaned backwards, then went flat on the floor, still mated with her, and she held on as if he was a lifeline.

He couldn't talk for a moment. She sighed and curled on top of him, holding him deep inside of her. At last he stirred and his eyes opened and he stared up at her.

She grinned, kissed his nose, her eyes sparkling with an unusual fire.

"You have any more surprises like that one, ex-cowboy now boy detective and Secret Service Agent?"

"Dozens, but I can only show you one a month. There have to be a few surprises down the line."

"You mean we have a 'down the line' to consider?" she asked looking at him quickly.

"Who knows. You might lose your voice tomorrow and I'd have to dump you."

She hit him in the side with her fist.

"Well, you might get called to Washington to take over the agency."

"Not a chance, there are six good men ahead of me."

"My tonsils are strong and my voice smooth. I'll still be singing this well in twenty years."

"Will you be making love this well?"

She smiled at him. "Why don't you hang around in my bed and see for yourself?"

"Always a chance," he said half seriously. Suddenly he grabbed her around the waist and lifted her body straight up off him and they slipped apart.

"Wine?" she asked.

"It's in your room. Want me to run up there bare assed and bring it back?"

She shook her head. "I'd rather have your bare ass in my bed."

They got off the floor and back in bed. He kissed her softly, then pushed her away.

"I wasn't kidding about one time only. I do have a damned tough job tomorrow, and I want to be ready for it."

"Oh, damn! Who can tell what's going to happen tomorrow? Maybe . . ." she stopped. "If I can't go to sleep, I might start to seduce you in your sleep."

"Fair enough," Spur said. He put one arm under the pillow under his head and put his other hand on his chest. It was his sleep position. In two minutes he was sleeping soundly.

Lila lay there for a while, then slid out of bed silently and lifted the big, heavy .45 six-gun from his holster. She held it for a minute. She carried it over to the bed and aimed the weapon at Spur's naked belly. She cocked the hammer back on a live round, then hesitated. Lila grinned as she remembered the marvelous way they had just made love and slid the big gun back in the holster where it hung over the wooden backed chair.

Maybe tomorrow they could make love again. What difference would another day make? She moved back into bed gently so she wouldn't wake him, reached over and put her hand over his genitals and soon drifted off to sleep.

Sometime during the night, Spur had a dream. He was running down a tunnel but couldn't see the end. Someone chased him with a dog on a leash that had a foaming mouth and huge teeth. The dog almost caught him and he turned and tried to fire his .45 at the dog, but a beautiful girl kept getting in the way and he never could fire.

He sat up, sweat wet on his forehead. Now what the hell was that all about? It had seemed so real. McCoy turned over, trying not to think about the dream. Tomorrow was going to be some of the toughest work he had ever done. He had to wrap up this case tomorrow, or he might never solve it!

17

Spur woke up with the sunrise and waited at the sheriff's office the next morning at 7:30 when the relief deputy came to work.

"Where's Galloway?" the lawman said.

"He's not feeling well. I told him to go home."

"You told . . ." the deputy stopped. "My name's Oberlin. Sheriff said you were some special kind of lawman. Guess we should get opened up for business."

Inside Spur moved toward the door that opened into the cells, then stopped. He looked at the deputy. "Oberlin, you're in charge of this office from now on. Last night the sheriff was murdered."

Oberlin scowled. "You're joshing me."

"No. There was a fire deliberately set. Galloway rushed out to help, the killer slipped inside and shot Frank. He's gone. I didn't even more him out of his cell. We should keep this to ourselves for a while. I want to look over the scene again."

Oberlin leaned against a desk.

"Frank Johnson is dead?"

"Sorry. I tried every trick I knew to protect him. I was simply outgunned." Spur went through the door into the cells and looked down at Frank. He concentrated on the letters crudely sketched on Frank's dark pants. Spur walked out to the office and brought back a pad of paper and a pencil. He copied down the writing as closely as he could.

It still came out a strong "L" and then from there on he wasn't sure. Best he could make out of it was a "D" or maybe an "E". The hand that had printed the letter in blood was shaky by that time. Frank had probably done it without looking down. Damn!

Deputy Oberlin came to the door and looked in.

"Christ, right in his bed! Who in hell . . . ?"

"That's what I'm going to find out, right now. How many men do you know who have the first initials of 'L' and either 'D' or 'E' for the last name? Make a list of them, right now. Your only job."

Spur turned back to the body. Again he went over the cell. There was no clue there, nothing had been dropped, no shell casing, no scrap of cloth or dropped cigarette or anything. He went out, closed the cell block door and headed to the street.

"I'm going to get the undertaker. His job now."

A half hour later the body had been taken out the back way and Spur looked over a list of names the deputy had made. There were only eight. Six of them were long time residents who hadn't been out of the county in years. The last two were possible, but one was a new Baptist preacher and the other one was the new owner of the struggling newspaper.

"Far as I know both those last two guys been in town the last few weeks. Both are real busy."

Nowhere, the initials had led him exactly nowhere. He stared down at the printing that he had copied from Frank's pants leg. What else could he make from it? Spur stared at the paper so long his vision blurred. He went out and walked the street, winding up at the undertaker. He walked inside.

The man was in back with the body. Spur went through the door and saw the man lifting something from Frank's belly wound. The undertaker turned and smiled.

"By damn, I found it!"

His name was Oliver. Spur didn't know if it was first or last or only. He held up something in bloody tweezers.

"Bullet that hurt him bad," Oliver said. "We used to call this a punishment round. Hurts like hell and will kill a man eventually, but makes him suffer for an hour to three hours. The worst kind of horrendous pain any human ever can stand."

Oliver wiped the lead slug off on a cloth, then washed it in a basin of water and dried it.

"I kept wondering why a belly shot with a big slug wouldn't go right through the body and out the back somewhere. Had a hunch, but now I got your answer. See this little cupping on the back of the slug?"

Spur looked closer and saw it. "Yeah."

Oliver took a .45 round off the table and with two pair of pliers carefully twisted the slug away from the copper casing. He turned it around so Spur could look at it.

"Same kind of cupping, right."

"True. What does that prove?"

Oliver tossed Spur another round from the table. It also was a .45 cartridge.

"That's a special load .45 round made especially for a weapon called the Aldrich. Actually a minor change in the standard derringer, but enough so it took a slightly shorter cartridge. They cupped the slug so they could get a little more powder in the charge. But it never was as powerful as the standard .45 round."

"A derringer? You're telling me that Frank Johnson was killed by a derringer slug?"

"Not sure. But this belly shot sure was. If I could find the other slug in one chunk it might prove it. But what killer is going to gut shoot his victim, then change guns for the heart shot?"

"A derringer. Now it makes sense. In a couple others I wondered why a muzzle blast like that wouldn't go right through a man and exit. They all were the same, and all derringer shots!" Spur leaned back against the wall. "This sets it up in a whole new light. It doesn't have to be a crazy outlaw who just got out of prison."

"Could be anybody," Oliver said. "Hell, I know a couple of women who carry little derringers for protection."

"A woman?" Spur asked himself. "Oh, my God!" Suddenly things tumbled into place, like the last few pieces of a giant jigsaw puzzle.

A woman. What person had been in the last two or three towns where lawmen were killed? What person had the opportunity to do the killings late at night? He thought of the initials again and took out the folded piece of paper from his pocket. What person he knew had a name that began with an "L"? He looked at the last wiggly lines he had copied. Damn! the last initial could have been not a "D" or an "E" but a "P."

Lila Pemberthy!

He shook his head and looked at the piece of paper again. There was no doubt, the first initial was plain, and the last one could be a "P." She had the opportunity. He had been with her at the last two towns!

"Don't tell anybody what you've found, Oliver. We might need this kind of evidence for a trial. I've got an idea who the killer is. Don't tell a soul!"

Spur walked quickly out of the death room and straight to the hotel. Lila was not in his room. He went up to her room and knocked. There was no response. She could be sleeping or having breakfast.

Spur used his pocket knife and pushed back the sliding bolt on the lock and slipped the door open. He swung it wide and stepped inside. She wasn't there. The bed was a mess and clothes were strewn everywhere. On the bed sat her large reticule. She had two or three of them.

Spur picked it up and noticed that it was heavy. He opened it and looked inside. The first thing he found was a derringer. He sniffed the barrels. It had been fired recently, he could still smell the cordite. Slowly he turned the weapon over and saw on the side the fancy scrolled name, "Aldrich."

He dropped down on the edge of the bed. He had never heard of the Aldrich. There might not be more than a hundred of them made. The coincidence was too great.

He smelled something. The weapon had another

odor on it but he couldn't place it. He opened the reticule again and lifted it to his nose.

The smell was unmistakable. Coal oil. A quart jar would fit neatly into the reticule. Just enough to get a house fire going so hot and fast burning that a local fire brigade couldn't put it out, and form the perfect diversion for a murder.

Spur put the reticule down and stared at the little gun. The shell casings were probably still in place. It was almost enough to charge her with murder, but not quite. All circumstantial. A jury liked to have an eye witness or a confession, or a lot more proof than he had.

"Good morning."

Spur looked up and saw Lila standing in the doorway. He hadn't thought to close it. "I see you've found my protection. A girl shouldn't be walking around a wild Western town like Dodge at night without some powerful personal protection."

Spur sighed. She was cool, cold, almost detached. She could do it. She had done it!

"This derringer isn't for protection, Lila, it's a murder weapon."

"Whatever do you mean?" She closed the door but stayed there leaning against it as she began to unbutton her dress top.

"Lila, why did you kill Sheriff Johnson?"

Her face flushed, her eyes blazed. "Because he killed my Robert!" The words screamed at him, rolling out of her mouth with ten years of pain and torment and anger and hatred. "Killed Robert and my Robert didn't do a thing to him. Kicked him in the head . . ." Her words had moderated, become normal speech tone, then faded to a whisper at the end.

She blinked and her face returned to its normal expression.

"Whatever do you mean the sheriff is dead?"

"This gun killed him, Lila, and I can prove it. It's a special weapon, not many were made. Takes a different kind of .45 round you can get only on order from the factory. And in your reticule are some spots of coal oil where the jar leaked. You used the coal oil to start the first last night, just before you slipped in and shot the sheriff to death."

"I don't understand . . ." The words trailed off, then her face changed, her eyes blazed and her hand darted into her reticule that hung from her wrist.

"See, Mr. Lawman. I have another derringer. They aren't so rare, I have two. And this one is loaded with two rounds. Oh, yes, I can use it. And keep your hand away from your weapon. I saw you kick my Robert to death. *I saw you!* Right there in the street! Half the town saw but they wouldn't lift a finger to help. Afraid of you. Everyone afraid!

"My Robert stood up to you and you called him a Texas Rebel bastard and you kicked him again. My Robert wasn't real strong. He was a prisoner during the war and he never was well after that. So you kicked him in the head! But that's the last good man you're ever gonna kill! You bastard!"

She rushed toward him. Spur knew the little derringers with its two-inch barrel was useless at more than two or three feet. He dove off the bed to the left as he heard the shot fire. It missed. He threw the derringer he held at her, saw her swing the weapon toward him again and fire as he hit the floor and rolled.

He felt the slug slam into the floor an inch from his side and wood splinters stabbed into his flesh. He rolled, came to his feet and caught Lila as she stumbled and fell on the bed. She still held the derringer.

She swept brown hair back out of her eyes and glared at him.

"Mr. Lawman, you done kicked my husband to death, and because of that I am going to have to kill you."

She put the still smoking derringer to Spur's belly and pulled the trigger. The firing pin fell on the spent round.

Her eyes were bright. "Now I'm going to remind you what you did to me and to my Robert.

"You slammed your gun down on his head and Robert fell into the dust. Poor Robert got to his knees, then struggled to stand. He was weaving, working hard just to stand up. But he stared hard at you, sheriff.

"He said, 'Suh, ah don't apologize to white trash like you!'

"Then you went crazy. Your big fist lashed out, hit poor Robert's chin and snapped his head back. He fell in the dirt in front of the hardware store. You bellowed something bout him being a Rebel. 'My kid brother got shot to death by bastards just like you in the war.' Then you kicked Robert in the side with your heavy boot. Robert curled in a ball.

"You dragged him to his feet, held his shirt front and pounded your fists into Robert's face again and again. Robert's nose spurted blood. You laughed. You closed one of his eyes and tore his ear. Robert's head flipped from side to side each time you hit him.

"I kept yelling at you to stop. Yelling for somebody to help us. But nobody came. A man and a woman on the boardwalk hurried past. A cowboy walking his horse down the street went to the far side and rode by quickly."

Spur held her as she screeched and roared at him. He sat there holding her from hitting him or hurting herself. She kept talking for five minutes. Telling him the story of how her Robert had been brutally killed by a Kansas sheriff in a street.

He had the idea that she gut shot her victims, made them listen to the story, then used the second round in the little gun to shoot them dead through the heart when they were helpless and half dead already.

Lila finished her story. She lifted her derringer and put it over Spur's heart, then she pulled the trigger. Again the firing pin struck a spent round.

She sat up then, put the derringer in her reticule and straightened her dress.

Lila Pemberthy looked at Spur and smiled.

"Hey, what are you doing in my bedroom? I didn't expect to see you until later today. You told me last night you had a lot of work to do."

She put her arms around his neck and kissed him tenderly, slowly, deliciously. Spur simply could not respond. He took her arms away.

"I have someone I want you to meet," he said.

She pushed against him, her breasts hard against his chest.

"We must have time for just once before we go. Please? You kind of promised last night."

Spur half relented. She was going to be in an institution somewhere for a long, long time.

"Maybe just one time." She grinned and straddled him, then moved to his right side and before he could react, she jerked his Colt .45 from the holster and tried to back away. He swept his heavy boot at her ankles, hitting them, tripping her. He saw her cocking the hammer as she fell. He dove on top of her, smashing her small body to the floor. Almost at the same instant the .45 roared.

Her eyes went wide and Lila gasped, then shuddered.

"Oh, God!" she said. "Oh, God, I shot myself!"

He rolled her over gently. Both her hands held her flat belly where a crimson stain already showed. The Colt lay to one side. Spur shoved it across the floor.

Somebody knocked on the door.

"Come in!" Spur shouted. A cowboy looked in.

"Thought I heard a shot . . . My God!"

"Run and get the doctor!" Spur bellowed.

The cowboy raced away and Spur could hear him tromping down the steps.

Lila looked up at him through the pain and the waves of nausea.

"Spur McCoy?"

"Yes, Lila. I'm right here." He held her head in his lap, and now bent and kissed her cheek.

"Did I tell you I'm going to Chicago next? I've got a job singing there at an opera house and the manager said they sometimes had a thousand people in the audience!" She coughed and blood tinged her lips.

"He said I could stay there two or three weeks. Isn't that great?"

"Yes. Robert would have been proud of you."

She frowned. "Robert? I don't know any Robert." Her face changed then and she bleated in pain and terror. "Spur, I hurt myself bad. I don't know even why I had a gun. I don't like guns. Why did I do that, Spur?"

"An accident, Lila. Just an accident. Nobody's to blame. I'll tell the deputy sheriff just what happened."

"Is a doctor coming?" She screamed then, a cry of pain and anger and fear, a wail of anguish that she had heard before from the string of gut shot lawmen she had watched die.

"It hurts so bad!"

"The doctor is coming, he'll help you get well."

Slowly she shook her head. She lifted her right hand. The whole hand dripped with blood.

"No. I understand how badly hurt I am. I'm . . . I'm going to be dead in less than an hour."

"You'll find Robert again," Spur said.

For a moment her face worked, then she smiled. "Yes, Robert. My first love, my husband. I was so young, only seventeen, but he was a war hero and so good to me. He defended me to the very last. Somewhere in Kansas he died. A terrible sheriff kicked him when he went down. And . . . and Robert never woke up." She sobbed.

The pain charged through her slender body again and she cried out in terror.

"I don't want to die!"

Three people came to the open door and looked in. Spur waved them away. The doctor hurried in and knelt beside her. He frowned when he saw the wound. He took her hand away and put a pad of cloth on her wound and pressed it tightly.

He shook his head at Spur when Lila couldn't see him.

"You just rest easy now, Miss. I've got something that will make you feel much better."

"No. Never feel better again. I understand, Doc. Go to somebody you can help. Not even laudanum would have time to make me feel better. Go on."

The doctor stood, then nodded. "You're a brave lady," he said and went out the door closing it behind him.

"Not brave, terrified!" she said.

"You'll see Robert again."

"Robert? I told you before, I don't know any Robert. I've never been religious. Dead is dead. I've never seen anybody come back to life. No proof there is anything more than what we have right here on the good earth. I tried to make it a happier place for those I sang for."

"You did that, Lila. You certainly did."

She gasped, closed her eyes as pain distorted her pretty face. In a moment it was over and she relaxed.

"Spur McCoy, kiss me."

He leaned down and pressed his lips to hers. When he lifted away he heard a long gush of air from her lungs. The lady avenger with the deadly derringer was dead.

Two days later Spur had completed all of his reports, filed all the proper papers with the county, and had his ticket on the morning stage east. He had named Lila as the sheriff's killer, told the whole story, and paid for her burial. Then he sent a long telegram to Washington giving the story in detail and closing out the deaths of the Kansas lawmen. That case was at last ended.

He was heading back to St. Louis. It had been more than six months since he had checked into his "office" there. He figured it was about time that he found out what the place looked like.

General Wilton Halleck, his boss in Washington and the second in command of the Secret Service Agency, had indicated there was a case coming up that would be bigger and wilder and more dangerous than anything he had ever tackled. The general would come to St. Louis in person to give Spur the assignment. He was to be well rested and ready before the general arrived.

Spur looked at the calendar on the wall. It was June 4. In three days he would be in St. Louis. The General was arriving on June 13. He would try his damnedest to be rested and ready by then. Curiousity billowed in him. He would just have to wait and see what this giant of an assignment was.

IF YOU ENJOYED THE ADVENTURES OF SPUR McCOY, BE SURE TO ORDER LEISURE'S RED-HOT *BUCKSKIN* SERIES

Make the Most of Your Leisure Time with
LEISURE BOOKS

Please send me the following titles:

Quantity	Book Number	Price
___	___	___
___	___	___
___	___	___
___	___	___

If out of stock on any of the above titles, please send me the alternate title(s) listed below:

___	___	___
___	___	___
___	___	___

Postage & Handling ___

Total Enclosed $ ___

☐ Please send me a free catalog.

NAME _____
(please print)

ADDRESS _____

CITY _____ STATE _____ ZIP_____

Please include $1.00 shipping and handling for the first book ordered and 25¢ for each book thereafter in the same order. All orders are shipped within approximately 4 weeks via postal service book rate. PAYMENT MUST ACCOMPANY ALL ORDERS.*

*Canadian orders must be paid in US dollars payable through a New York banking facility.

Mail coupon to: **Dorchester Publishing Co., Inc.**
6 East 39 Street, Suite 900
New York, NY 10016
Att: ORDER DEPT.